"Celebrate?" Laura wondered what Sam meant.

He brushed her cheek with his fingertip. "Not what you think, although it's worth consideration."

Laura tried to be nonchalant, but her body warmed just being in Sam's arms. "Are you saying I'm safe with you?"

"For now." His wicked grin belied his words.

"You'll warn me if things change?" she asked.

Sam sat down and put his arms behind him. "Look, you could do anything to me, and I won't touch you."

Laura's gaze locked with is. "Anything?"

"Anything."

Gathering her courage, Laura brushed his cheek the way he'd brushed hers. He didn't blink. She bent to his upturned face and kissed his mouth. When she felt his lips respond to hers, she drew back. "Maybe that's enough for now."

"Yes," he agreed in a throaty voice that told her he was just as affected by the kiss as she was.

She gazed at him quizzically, wondering where to go from here.

Dear Reader,

Welcome to Harlequin American Romance, where you're guaranteed upbeat and lively love stories set in the backyards, big cities and wide-open spaces of America.

Kick-starting the month is an AMERICAN BABY selection by Mollie Molay. The hero of *The Baby in the Back Seat* is one handsome single daddy who knows how to melt a woman's guarded heart! Next, bestselling author Mindy Neff is back with more stories in her immensely popular BACHELORS OF SHOTGUN RIDGE series. In *Cheyenne's Lady*, a sheriff returns home to find in his bed a pregnant woman desperate for his help. Honor demands that he offer her his name, but will he ever give his bride his heart?

In *Millionaire's Christmas Miracle*, the latest book in Mary Anne Wilson's JUST FOR KIDS miniseries, an abandoned baby brings together a sophisticated older man who's lost his faith in love and a younger woman who challenges him to take a second chance on romance and family. Finally, don't miss Michele Dunaway's *Taming the Tabloid Heiress*, in which an alluring journalist finesses an interview with an elusive millionaire who rarely does publicity. Exactly how *did* the reporter get her story?

Enjoy all four books—and don't forget to come back again in December when Judy Christenberry's *Triplet Secret Babies* launches Harlequin American Romance's continuity MAITLAND MATERNITY: TRIPLETS, QUADS & QUINTS, and Mindy Neff brings you another BACHELORS OF SHOTGUN RIDGE installment.

Wishing you happy reading,

Melissa Jeglinski
Associate Senior Editor
Harlequin American Romance

THE BABY IN THE BACK SEAT
Mollie Molay

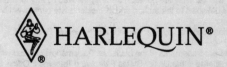

TORONTO • NEW YORK • LONDON
AMSTERDAM • PARIS • SYDNEY • HAMBURG
STOCKHOLM • ATHENS • TOKYO • MILAN • MADRID
PRAGUE • WARSAW • BUDAPEST • AUCKLAND

To the Baby's godmothers, Betty, Joan, Aline, Linda and Ann and RisaLee for ten long years of friendship.

ISBN 0-373-16897-7

THE BABY IN THE BACK SEAT

ABOUT THE AUTHOR

After working for a number of years as a logistics contract administrator in the aircraft industry, Mollie Molay turned to a career she found far more satisfying—writing romance novels. Mollie lives in Northridge, California, surrounded by her two daughters and eight grandchildren, many of whom find their way into her books. She enjoys hearing from her readers and welcomes comments. You can write to her at Harlequin Books, 300 East 42nd St., 6th Floor, New York, NY 10017.

Books by Mollie Molay

HARLEQUIN AMERICAN ROMANCE
560—FROM DRIFTER TO DADDY
597—HER TWO HUSBANDS
616—MARRIAGE BY MISTAKE
638—LIKE FATHER, LIKE SON
682—NANNY & THE BODYGUARD
703—OVERNIGHT WIFE
729—WANTED: DADDY
776—FATHER IN TRAINING
799—DADDY BY CHRISTMAS
815—MARRIED BY MIDNIGHT
839—THE GROOM CAME C.O.D.
879—BACHELOR-AUCTION BRIDEGROOM
897—THE BABY IN THE BACK SEAT

Dear Reader,

My father used to say children were life's dividends, and grandchildren were bonuses.

The first time I fell in love with my own little dividend was when my first daughter, Elaine, was put into my arms. When my second little dividend was born, I named her Joy. Because that's what she and her sister were and are to me.

My grandchildren, my little bonuses, have brought love, laughter and meaning into my life. Although most children learn to walk, talk and give hugs, when mine did, it seemed unique.

I've included each of them and their exploits in each of my stories in some way. There is an Annie, and I hope you enjoy her as much as I do.

Mollie Molay

Prologue

Sam Harrison stood in front of the house and gazed stoically at the SOLD banner nailed across the FOR SALE sign on the manicured green lawn. The small three-bedroom tract home wasn't a mansion by any stretch of the imagination, but he'd been proud to present it to Paige as a wedding gift. Too bad his flight-attendant wife had been more excited about gaining a slot on a Denver-to-London flight than about having a home.

Living solo hadn't been very rewarding. Thursday he'd been in Europe, Friday in Florida, and today he was home in Colorado. Except he had no home anymore.

Fifteen months ago he'd been happily married.

Fourteen months ago he'd learned he was to be a father.

Six months ago baby Annie came into the world and crept into his heart at first glance.

He'd been hurt, even humiliated at the divorce, but it was all his fault. He should have taken the time to find out if Paige had a nesting instinct, not an unfulfilled case of wanderlust.

The unexpected arrival of an infant daughter had been another gift that hadn't pleased his ex-wife for long. The "friendly skies" still seemed to hold a greater charm than motherhood.

He didn't mind losing the house, nor, now that he was able to think of it more dispassionately, did he mind the divorce. After Paige had announced their marriage had been a mistake, he'd taken no pleasure in staying where he wasn't wanted. It was losing out at fatherhood that hurt.

After being persuaded a newborn baby was better off with her mother, it had been leaving Annie, a small part of himself, that broke his heart.

His ex-wife appeared in the doorway. "Good. You're just in time. The movers will be here any moment."

Sam took a deep breath and strode to meet her. "Sorry. I would have shown up sooner, but I had an assignment to finish."

"You always have an assignment to finish," she answered with a shrug. "Come on in—this won't take long. I have your things here inside the door."

Sam followed her into the house and briefly

thought of the broken dreams the house represented. "I'll leave as soon as I say goodbye to Annie."

Under Paige's watchful eye, he went into the bedroom where Annie was sleeping on her back with a tiny finger in her rosebud mouth. She looked so peaceful he didn't have the heart to wake her. Instead, he tucked the blanket closer around her tiny shoulders and leaned over to place a kiss on her forehead. He held his breath when Annie stirred. For a hopeful moment Sam thought she was about to open her eyes. Instead, a frown appeared on her forehead, and she fell back to sleep.

Paige lingered by the doorway. "You really go for this fatherhood bit, don't you?"

Sam swallowed the lump that threatened to undermine his reluctant acceptance of the status quo. He'd wanted to be a father from the moment he'd lost his own father as a young boy. A loving father who would be there for his child. To watch over his child in good times and in bad and to give it the security he hadn't been lucky enough to know himself.

For too short a time marriage to Paige and Annie's arrival seemed to fulfill that dream. As for leaving Annie, he understood a baby needed to be with her mother, but at least he'd gotten visiting rights. Maybe even weekend custody or holidays when she grew older.

Ignoring Paige's comment, he took in the heart-shaped baby face, the golden-brown eyelashes, the tendrils of light-brown hair and the tiny lips that had accepted him without question. What would he do without her?

He turned to look at Paige. "Can't we stay friends? For Annie's sake if not our own?"

Paige hesitated, glanced at the sleeping baby. "Sure, I guess."

With a last look at his infant daughter, Sam straightened. "Thanks. By the way, you will let me know when you get to your mother's, won't you? I'd like to made some arrangements to see Annie as often as I can."

His ex-wife shrugged. "Sure."

Sam went to the door, lifted a box that contained some of his personal belongings and headed for his rental car just as a moving van drove up. "I'll be back in a minute," he said over his shoulder. "I want to make sure I get the photography equipment I left in the garage." Paige went into the house.

Fifteen minutes later Sam reappeared around the front of the house with a box in his arms. The rest of his belongings and his suitcase had been moved. Paige stood by the side of his SUV.

"I had one of the movers put your things in the

car for you,'' she said, and held out her hand. ''I guess this is goodbye.''

''Thanks,'' he answered dryly as he shook her hand. With a last regretful glance at the house, he got into the SUV, waved once and drove away.

Chapter One

A baby cried.

Clicking off the car radio, Sam peered anxiously at the map furnished by the car-rental agency in Grand Junction and frowned. He didn't know what bothered him more: finding himself on an unmarked county road or the unwelcome reminder he'd left his infant daughter behind with his ex-wife a few hours ago.

As much as he would have liked to be a real father, he'd never managed to spend more than an hour or two with Annie. First, because he'd never felt welcome in his own home, and second, because his obsession with photography kept getting in the way. Which condition had contributed to his divorce was beyond him, but this proposed shared custody when Annie was older twisted in his gut.

He consoled himself with the thought that he'd be able to see the baby between assignments. And that when she got old enough for him to care for, he'd call in his shared-custody rights. Until then, she was better off with someone who knew how to take care of her.

Suddenly aware he should have been at his destination by now, his thoughts turned to the immediate problem.

As a photojournalist, he'd flown, driven and hiked to more offbeat and secluded places than he could count. He'd won half-a-dozen awards for his photo stories and had the trophies to prove it. Heck, he was even an internationally known photojournalist.

Until today, he'd managed to find his way around without a problem. So how in hell had he managed to get himself lost on a dirt road on the western slopes of the Colorado Rockies?

He didn't really mind getting lost, he told himself as he peered out the window, trying to pinpoint his present location. The surrounding terrain was beautiful and so photogenic his fingers itched to grab his camera. He'd start shooting the miles of fresh green grass that, after last night's rain, glistened in the afternoon sun. Or he'd capture the shadows cast by the ragged mountains just beyond the horizon.

Too bad he'd packed his cameras in the back, he thought wryly. He couldn't reach one without pulling off the road and rummaging through the boxes packed on the back seat of the car. Or in the cargo space, which was full of his belongings.

With a rain-soaked dirt road under the wheels, capturing on film the majestic green peaks was tempting, but it would have to wait until he reached his destination. If ever.

Getting lost really bothered him. Losing control. He was a man who wrote his own rules, traveled when, where and how he wanted and lived the good life. In his book, that meant being in charge.

To his growing disgust, he wasn't in charge now.

In the background, he heard a baby whimper.

Sam frowned and checked the car radio. It wasn't on. With a shrug he laid the sound down to an overactive imagination triggered by a guilt trip at having driven away from the one person he loved more than life itself—Annie.

The baby whimpered again, a demand for attention if he'd ever heard one, he thought miserably as he glanced through the rearview mirror.

The sight of the back of an infant car seat buckled on the back seat sent his adrenaline into overdrive.

A baby? Annie? If this was Paige's idea of a joke, it was a damn poor one.

His attention momentarily diverted, the large white rented SUV bumped into a pothole, slid and, to his mounting horror, shot across a narrow ditch and aimed straight for an ancient weathered fence.

His heart thundered as he threw all of his 180 pounds into stomping on the brakes. To his mounting dismay, the car skidded on the muddy road and continued on its wayward course straight for the fence.

Cursing his luck, Sam broke into a cold sweat. A giant stab of pain tore at his forehead. Terror washed over him as he realized the wheels had no traction. Heaven only knew where he would wind up. Or, if he was lucky, that the SUV would end up in one piece.

It wasn't himself he was thinking about—it was the baby in the back seat he'd heard crying. He gritted his teeth.

Instead of coming to a stop, the SUV tore through the fence rails, careered up a small slope and crashed into a small water tower, with predictable results. As if in slow motion, the tower swayed, toppled and showered the car with a torrent of water. With a muffled curse, he wrested the door open, bounded out and headed for the rear door to rescue the baby in the back seat.

The baby was indeed Annie, and she was demanding attention in the only way she knew how. Tears rolled down her pink cheeks. Hiccups shook her tiny frame. To his relief she opened her eyes and smiled through her tears when she saw him.

Shielding her from the water with his body, Sam

hurried to unfasten the baby carrier, grabbed it in his arms and stumbled away from the soaked SUV to dry land.

Annie's brown eyes, golden-brown hair and teary smile brought a lump to his throat and questions to his mind. How had Annie gotten into the SUV?

A close look revealed a note pinned to her blanket.

"Sam," he read with dismay, "I saw the way you looked at Annie when you said goodbye. I realized then she was better off with you than with me. By the time you read this, I'll be on my way to Paris. Don't bother to call me. I'll call you. Paige."

His heart beat double-time as he realized this was the reason Paige had been so anxious to help him load his belongings and to send him on his way.

He managed to muster a smile to reassure his infant daughter. There was no use scaring her, he thought as he regarded tiny teeth between quivering lips. A little dimple on her chin, a duplicate of his own larger one, clinched the deal. Annie was his responsibility.

Annie had been the unplanned result of a brief visit home fifteen months ago. Because of his commitments, he'd only seen her twice since she'd been born six months ago. Once, when she was born and her mother had shocked him by telling him she planned a divorce. The second, a few short hours ago when he'd kissed Annie goodbye.

His heart finally slowed enough so he could take a deep breath. It wasn't only the accident that gave him pause. It was the thought of taking on the responsibility of raising a child on his own. Especially one as young as Annie.

One thing for sure, fatherhood had to be a daunting experience under any circumstances.

In his case, he honestly knew zip about babies. If Annie didn't fit into her mother's schedule, she didn't fit into his own nomadic career, either.

He gazed at his infant daughter. She might have been unplanned and her presence in the SUV unexpected, but he loved every tiny inch of her.

His lifestyle was definitely going to have to change.

His immediate problem, aside from having Annie with him, was the car's busted radiator. He wasn't going anywhere anytime soon.

He took a deep breath to calm his nerves and smiled his reassurance at the baby. Good thing she couldn't know he hadn't the foggiest idea of what to do now. Not with her or the car, either.

Shouts, the excited barking of a dog and the sound of a galloping horse drew his attention. In the distance he saw a rider bearing down on him. Thank

God, he thought as he jiggled the baby carrier; help was on its way.

He drew a deep breath and fought to think of a lucid answer to the question that was surely coming. What in hell had caused him to crash through the fence and take down the water tower?

A baby's cry? No one in his right mind would believe him. After all, from his limited experience he knew babies cried all the time.

He hadn't known the baby was there? How could he explain he hadn't known Annie was in the back seat until he heard her cry? True, but no one would buy that story, either.

Explain that his ex-wife must have put the baby in the SUV while he was picking up the last of his belongings and about to leave home for the last time? That was the truth but just as unbelievable.

The rider bore down on him. There was something about the guy's body language that told him not to expect a welcome. He clutched the baby carrier and took a step back.

"Just what did you think you were doing?" the irate rider shouted. He pulled the horse to a halt inches away from Sam's nose and glared down at him.

Sam swallowed hard. He didn't blame the guy for being angry, but the look on his face was more than anger. The guy was furious.

"Sorry, mister," Sam began, then stopped short when he realized the person confronting him was a woman. And not an ordinary woman. This one had a rifle resting in the crook of her elbow and looked ready to use it.

He did a double take and took another step backward. He couldn't help himself. Up close the woman looked interesting, if dangerous. She was dressed in a well-washed blue cotton shirt and tight worn jeans. Long trim legs were encased in soft leather boots that, like the ranch behind her, had seen better days. From her boots to her gold windblown hair, she was all woman. A woman with sparkling green eyes that would have reminded him of green meadows in springtime if she hadn't been so angry. Right now, her eyes looked like twin tornadoes.

Her eyes widened when she finally focused on the infant carrier in his arms. She let loose with the barrage of questions he'd known were coming. "What in heaven's name were you thinking? How could you drive so irresponsibly with a baby in the car?" Before he could answer, she went on, "Is the baby all right? You're lucky the two of you weren't killed!"

"I didn't know she was there," Sam protested when the woman stopped to catch her breath. He straightened his back and attempted a smile. What was he apologizing for? After all, he was innocent.

"That is, I didn't know she was there until I heard her cry. Her crying startled me and made me lose control of the car."

Behind him, the last wooden support of the water tower fell with a thud, and the last of the water it had contained drained out like a creek that had broken through its banks.

Sam and the woman on the horse surveyed the scene in silence. He was trying to think of something to say when she spoke for him. "Great driving," she finally said with a look of disgust.

Sam had intended to try to charm his way through the confrontation, but it was obviously no use. The lady was mad as hell at the destruction of her property. He looked back over his shoulder at the muddy tire skids, the broken fence, the pile of wood and corrugated tin that had been a water tower. Considering the amount of devastation he'd caused, he couldn't blame her. He hoped she had no thoughts of using the gun she held. "Don't worry. I'll pay for the damages."

"You didn't know the baby was there?" she echoed, ignoring his offer. Her eyes narrowed, and she studied him closely. Close enough to make him shiver under his soaked clothing, even though the sun was shining. "Been drinking?"

"No way!" Sam answered, juggling the carrier so that Annie wouldn't think he'd forgotten her.

"The God's honest truth is that my ex-wife put the baby in the back seat of my car without telling me."

"Try again," his inquisitor said dryly. "Sounds like a custody argument to me. Are you sure you didn't take the baby when your ex wasn't looking?"

Sam was insulted. He'd been called a lot of things, but never anything as bad as this. "Good Lord! Do I look like a kidnapper?"

When the woman raised an eyebrow, Sam felt like a fool. She was right. He might not look like a kidnapper, but he did look foolish.

Between the damaged SUV, his own wet and muddy condition, the baby in the carrier and the woman on horseback holding a gun, things were beginning to look like a TV sitcom. Only he didn't feel like laughing.

"It's the truth. When I stopped to pick up my belongings at my ex's request, Paige must have put the baby carrier with Annie into the car. I swear, this came as a complete surprise."

The rider's raised eyebrows suggested her disbelief, but he was beyond caring. It was beginning to look as if this mishap could wind up as a case of life or death. Or jail.

He was ready to admit that in his case truth *was* stranger than fiction. He might be innocent of kidnapping, but he sure hoped smashing a fence and a water tower weren't shooting offenses around here.

Now that she'd cooled down, Laura had to bite her lip to smother a laugh. The man's story was too ridiculous to be a fabrication, but it didn't get him off the hook. The damage he'd caused couldn't have come at a worse time. She silently surveyed the destruction. Repairing the fence and putting up a new water tower would set her back months if he didn't have the funds to do the job. She saw hundreds of dollars, maybe thousands, in repairs facing her. Money she didn't have and wasn't likely to borrow in time to prevent the loss of her herd, small though it was.

As for the baby smiling at her from the infant seat, she definitely had her father's coloring and, in any case, was too cute to ignore. From the way things looked, she was in need of some tender loving care.

Laura studied the baby's father. She'd been around men long enough to sense he was a man's man, even if he didn't know how to drive. He was larger than life, handsome, tall and lithe. A brown-and-white shirt was stretched taut across his chest. Long legs were encased in stone-washed jeans and ended in brown leather boots. His clear chocolate-brown eyes, so like the baby's, met hers in a way that made her all too aware of him. So what if his glance and the muscular chest showing under his wet shirt warmed her middle? She had more important things to think about than a sexy man.

Keeping her mind on saving the ranch from being sold from under her was her number-one priority, and he wasn't helping.

She smothered a sigh. Whatever the outcome of his unexpected arrival, the stranger was someone she wouldn't easily forget after he was gone. As for the baby...well, she couldn't afford to dwell on her, either.

"Who are you, and where did you think you were going?"

"The name is Sam Harrison," he answered. "I'm a photojournalist. Actually I was on my way to photograph the New Horizons Spa when I managed to get lost." He gestured to the sodden road map lying in the mud at his feet. "According to the map the car-rental agency gave me, the spa should have been somewhere around here."

It wasn't the first time some tenderfoot had gotten lost on his way to the spa. She was used to strangers driving up to her door expecting a glamorous health spa instead of a run-down sheep ranch. But it was the first time anyone had managed to trash her property in the process. Frowning, she swallowed an angry retort and gazed at the unhappy culprit. "You took the wrong turn at the crossroads about two miles back."

The baby cried again. Sam unbuckled the infant carrier, took the baby in his arms and tried to soothe her. To his chagrin, her bottom was damper than the tears that lingered in the corner of her eyes. He felt like a heel. No wonder the poor kid had been crying her heart out for attention. What kind of father did that make him?

"What do you intend to do now?" the rider asked.

"Beats me." He glanced at the busted SUV and ran his fingers through the shock of hair that fell over his forehead. "Outside of calling the rental agency, I haven't a clue."

"Try." She gestured to the fallen water tower, now a limp mass of corrugated tin, and the pieces of fencing scattered over the road. "And while you're thinking, don't forget to figure out how you're going to pay for the damage you caused. Without a fence, my livestock can wander out onto the road. That is, if they don't die of thirst first."

That caught Sam's attention. "Good Lord! You can't possibly mean it's as bad as all that!"

He looked horrified, but she didn't take the time to explain. The sheep wouldn't die of thirst, not after a spring storm that had left pockets of water standing in the meadow, but they would undoubtedly head for greener pastures if the fence wasn't fixed soon. What she'd told him came too close to the truth for her own peace of mind.

She leaned on the pommel of the saddle. "Every word, Mr. Harrison. Hope you can afford it, because repairing the fence and replacing the water tower at double time are going to cost you a bundle."

"Don't worry. I told you I'll take care of it." He felt in his back pocket, then shrugged. "I'll give you a check as soon as I get someplace dry." He held the baby away from the damp spot on his shirt and mustered a weak grin. "I'll have to find a motel where I can clean us up."

Laura eyed him thoughtfully and relaxed her vigilance. The guy was a lousy driver, but she'd bet her last dollar he was honest. She would have sent him packing after he wrote her a check, but the SUV clearly wasn't going anywhere. Besides, there was a baby to consider.

First things first. She gestured to the ranch house behind her. "I'm Laura Evans, and this my ranch, the Lazy E. As for a motel, there aren't any. Not around here, anyway."

Obviously dismayed, Sam eyed her. His grin faded. "You've got to be kidding! There are motels everywhere. Except maybe when you need them," he added with a distracted look around. "I guess we can bunk in the SUV until help comes."

Laura's conscience stirred. The man needed help,

and his infant daughter definitely looked as if she needed some attention. What could it hurt if she took them in for a few hours while he waited for a tow truck?

She gestured over her shoulder. "My place back there is the only building around for miles. If you like, you can follow me and get yourself and your daughter cleaned up before you move on."

"Move on? I wish." He gestured at the banged-up SUV sitting in the mud. To Laura it looked like a drowned duck with its nose stuck in the mud and its rear end in the air. "I don't think I'll be able to go anywhere for a while." He sighed and gently rocked the baby. "But if it's okay with you, I'd like to take you up on your offer. First I have to make a telephone call."

"Local?"

"Don't worry, I have a cell phone."

Satisfied, Laura nodded. "Want to hand me the baby? You can follow me to the ranch house when you're ready."

He pointedly eyed the rifle and the dog poised at attention at her feet and shook his head. "No thanks. I'll carry her." As an afterthought, he added, gesturing to the rifle, "Had some trouble around here?"

Laura met his gaze. "You don't have to worry. I've been bothered by a couple of unsavory characters lately and had to run them off. I wasn't sure you weren't more of the same. Or if you'd been sent to deliberately wreck the fence and the water tower to harass me.''

''Harass you? What for?''

''To get me to sell the ranch.''

Without taking his gaze off the rifle, he nodded warily. ''You're not planning on using that, are you?''

She leaned on the pommel of the saddle and looked him squarely in the eyes until he squirmed. ''Should I be?''

Sam shuddered. ''I told you the truth. I'm a photojournalist. I shoot with a camera, not with a gun. In fact, I'd feel a heck of a lot better about all this if you'd put that thing away.''

''No problem.'' She slid the rife into the leather scabbard attached to the saddle. The dog poised at the horse's feet relaxed, but to add to Sam's discomfiture, continued to eye him warily. ''So do I get the baby? Looks to me as if you have enough on your hands without her.''

''Her name is Annie,'' he said. He tramped back to the SUV and reached inside for the diaper bag that had been sitting beside the car seat. Back on dry land, he handed the bag and the baby to Laura. ''Whatever her mother had in mind when she stashed Annie in my car, I hope she remembered to provide the fixings for Annie's care.'' He managed a grin. "Too bad she didn't take the time to explain what I need to do with them."

Laura whistled at the watchful dog. "Don't worry, your daughter is in good hands. I'll take care of her for now. Make your call, and follow me when you're ready."

While he punched out the number of the car-rental agency in Grand Junction on his cell, Sam watched Laura Evans canter off with Annie in her arms. In spite of his dim view of women at the moment, he couldn't help but feel attracted to the feisty rancher.

To his disgust, he was put on hold, but this time he didn't get as steamed as he usually did. The wait gave him time to check out the way Laura Evans filled out her form-fitting jeans and cotton shirt. He actually admired the picture she made—until he thought about the reason she carried a rifle.

He glanced at the weathered buildings, the lack of any real activity that bespoke a successful ranch. If the lady's property was a paying proposition, it would be a surprise to him.

It looked as if Laura Evans ought to make the best of the situation and sell out to the highest bidder, instead of threatening would-be buyers with a rifle.

Someone finally answered his telephone call. He swore under his breath at the reply and put the phone

back in his pocket. He wasn't going anywhere, at
least no time soon.

Shivering, he reached into the SUV for his duffel
bag. Considering his dripping shirt and jeans and
muddy boots, Annie wasn't the only one who
needed changing.

He knew he had to find a way to move on once
he and Annie were clean and dry. Maybe calling the
spa and asking for transportation would work. Sure
as hell, if someone was trying to harass Laura Evans
or frighten her into selling her ranch, the last thing
she needed was to have him and Annie around to
add to her problems. And the last thing *he* needed
was to become involved.

As far as he could tell, paying for the damage
he'd caused wasn't going to help Laura Evans, either. Considering the mess it sounded she was in,
what the lady needed was a miracle.

Chapter Two

Sam locked the banged-up SUV and, with a last rue-ful glance at the broken fence, trudged through the mud and up the small rise to the ranch house. From what he could see, the only tall structure around had been the water tower. Just his luck.

Outside of a weathered barn and a few newly painted small cabins, the redwood-sided ranch house was the only building worth a damn, in his opinion. Judging from a recent coat of oil-based stain, some-one must have paid some attention to putting the place in shape. A futile effort if ever there was one, but he had to admire the effort. A dozen sheep grazed in a distant meadow. If they were the extent of the Evans herd, no wonder she was in trouble.

He noticed newly planted rosebushes ringing the porch as he approached the house. Stones, painted white, lined the freshly raked walk. Alongside the house, two lawn swings sat under the shade of an oak tree. The only sign of life was an elderly cow-hand busy assembling what appeared to be some kind of wooden jungle gym.

A jungle gym? Sam gazed around for a sign of kids. Outside of the cowboy and the dog now sprawled on the porch watching him closely, there wasn't another soul in sight. He shrugged and continued squishing his way in his muddy boots to the ranch house.

Not bad, he thought as he trudged up the wooden steps. Children or not, at least someone cared enough about the place to try to make it look decent.

The interior of the house, as he stood behind a screen door gazing in, surprised him even more. In contrast to the worn exterior, comfortable maple furniture had been burnished to a mellow yellow-brown sheen. Inviting rose-and-sea-foam-green chintz pillows had been thrown onto a large upholstered couch protected by crocheted white doilies. Hand-hooked rugs blanketed the polished oak floor in front of the couch. A huge stone fireplace covered a wall. Two comfortable-looking armchairs were drawn up in front of the fireplace. Sam sighed. The room looked mighty inviting after the accident and shower he'd just endured.

It was the kind of setting his mother and grand-mother would have appreciated. In fact, he would have enjoyed a home like this if his profession hadn't kept him on the move. And if he'd had a wife to welcome him home.

He glanced up to see Laura standing at the door and watching him expectantly. "What?"

"You've forgotten something." She gestured to his mud-caked boots. "Please take off your boots and leave them by the door before you come in."

Hopping on one foot at a time, Sam managed to comply. To his disgust, even his socks were soaked. Under Laura's watchful gaze, he took them off, dropped them and his boots outside the door and gingerly entered the house barefoot. Damn, he thought, there was something about not having his boots on that put him at a clear disadvantage.

"Are you ready for Annie?"

Sam felt himself flush at the reminder of his daughter. He would have offered to clean up the baby before now, except he didn't have a clue what to do. He not only felt inadequate, but he also didn't like the reproachful look in Laura's eyes. So what if he didn't know about the care and feeding of babies? Were all fathers supposed to have learned how to diaper a baby, or did it come naturally?

"Sure, but..." He tried to look cool, but the truth was unavoidable. Maybe things would have been different if Paige had stuck around long enough to give him a chance. "I'm afraid I've never diapered a baby before."

Laura didn't look surprised. "I guess you're not part of the seventy percent of today's fathers who help raise their children."

If there was one thing sure to light Sam's fire, it was being put on the defensive. Especially when he felt that, under the circumstances, he was innocent of any blame. "Where did you get a statistic like that?"

"I was a maternity-ward nurse before I came back home to take care of my folks. We took a poll at the hospital and that's what we found. Most men today say family comes first. In fact, some choose to stay at home with their children while their wives go out to work."

Sam tried to envision staying behind to take care of home, hearth and family while Paige flew to Paris and points unknown. Considering how little he knew about the requirements of a house husband, let alone a father, the picture that came to mind was so ludicrous he almost laughed.

He focused on one thing Laura had said that calmed him. A maternity-ward nurse? His spirits rose. This was the first bit of good news he'd had all day. "You're not putting me on, are you? A real maternity-ward nurse?"

"Until two years ago," she answered. "I came back to stay when my parents passed away. So if you have any intention of raising your daughter by yourself, maybe you ought to let me show you how to care for her, instead of doing it for you."

"Go ahead, please. Teach me."

With a wry glance at Sam, Laura took a changing pad, wipes and a fresh diaper out of the diaper bag. She knelt on the floor beside the coffee table. "Watch carefully," she said as she undid Annie's soggy diaper. Crooning to the baby, she laid her on the pad. "First off you have to remember to change her often. A baby's skin is very sensitive." Sam nodded. "Actually," she went on as she used a wipe to dry off Annie's little bottom before she set a new diaper in place, "you're lucky Annie is a girl. You have to work faster if the baby's a boy."

Sam edged closer and cautiously surveyed the process. As far as he was concerned, regardless of sex, a diaper change was a diaper change. How difficult could it be? "Yeah?"

"Little boys are like fountains," she answered. She applied talcum powder, and Annie giggled. "If you don't want an unexpected shower, you have to take precautions and move fast."

Sam flushed. The last thing he'd ever expected to do was discuss a baby's plumbing with a woman he found intriguing.

It wasn't only Laura Evans's appearance that interested him—although she certainly wasn't lacking in the looks department. It was her cool command under fire, coupled with her smile and warmth when it came to Annie that made him take a closer look at her.

He'd met, photographed and romanced a number of desirable women in his time—as a single man, of course. He'd even been fool enough to marry one of them: Paige. He'd been so taken with Paige, he hadn't stopped to consider she was a woman bent on adventure, not on being matrimonial material.

But nowhere had he met a multifaceted woman like Laura. He was willing to bet she ran her ranch with the same skill she'd demonstrated as a nurse. And from what he'd seen of the house, she was probably just as good at nesting as she was at her profession.

Things might have been different if he hadn't had his fill of beautiful women.

Mental warning bells sounded as one warm thought followed another. After his sorry marital experience, why was he even mulling over what made Laura Evans tick? Or thinking of her in a romantic way? Hadn't he already decided there was no way a man could begin to understand women, let alone try to live with one? That it was better to look and admire but not touch? Nesting women could be dangerous to a man like him. He drew a deep breath and gazed around the room. ''Interesting place you have here.''

Laura pulled the baby's romper over the fresh diaper and snapped the crotch. Instead of handing the baby over to its father, she buried her nose in the baby's neck and made bubbling noises. Not only because she couldn't resist hearing Annie laugh, but also because playing with the baby was the only way she could think of to keep her mind off Annie's father.

Sam Harrison, bare feet, wet clothing and all, was the masculine type of man who rang her bell. The fact that he obviously loved his infant daughter and, although he knew zip about babies, was ready to raise her by himself made him more of a man than most in her eyes. That was the trouble. The last thing she needed in her life right now was a baby she couldn't keep or a wandering man like Sam Harrison. A man who made her think of dreams best forgotten.

A baby had been her dream from the time a sympathetic foster mother had handed her her first doll. A hand-me-down doll with faded clothing and one eye missing, the doll had been her pride and joy. She'd built an imaginary family around Dolly Dimples and dreamed of a day when she would have her own children. A dream that had been shattered when, as a newly adopted thirteen-year-old, she'd been thrown from a horse and suffered internal injuries. Injuries that would prevent her from becoming a mother.

Laura closed her eyes, gave Annie one last hug and reluctantly handed the baby back to her father. "Diapering isn't the only task you'll have to master if you intend to care for Annie by yourself."

Jolted from his musings, Sam forced his thoughts from what made his reluctant hostess tick to his present problem. For sure he'd better get his act together and learn all he could about taking care of Annie while he had the chance. "Right. Maybe you can show me a few other tricks before I leave."

Her answering frown told him he was skating on thin ice. Maybe "tricks" hadn't been the best description for baby care he could have used. The way Laura was looking at him told him he was on probation as a father. He hurried to change the topic.

"By the way, the car-rental agency told me it's going take a few days before they can get me another car. Seems there's some sort of local holiday going on."

Laura nodded. "Miners' Days celebration."

"Right. From the sound of it, I'm afraid I might have to stick around here until they can bring an SUV from Denver." Laura's frown grew deeper, but this would give Sam the time to learn how to take care of Annie. "The rental agency offered to reimburse me for my room and board until they arrive,'' he added hopefully. ''How about it? Can we stay?''

Laura fought her pride and lost. She knew having Sam Harrison and little Annie around would be treading on dangerous territory for more than one reason. But bottom line, she needed the money.

''I'd planned on taking in campers to make the ranch pay, but not the adult kind,'' she replied. And certainly not a man who appealed to her senses as strongly as Sam Harrison did. Not that she didn't welcome Annie's presence, she did. But not Annie's father.

She didn't want to wind up caring about Sam Harrison. She knew all too well there was no future in it for either of them.

She finally nodded. ''I'll let you know what it will cost to replace the water tower and to mend the fence. As for your staying here, pay whatever you think is fair.''

Sam juggled Annie in one arm and pulled out his wallet. It was a struggle, but he managed to get it and to hand Laura two one-hundred-dollar bills. ''That ought to do it for now.'' When she hesitated, he hurried to add, ''Go ahead, take it. The car-rental agency will reimburse me.'' When she hesitated, he added another hundred. ''That's for taking care of Annie.''

''The care of Annie is on the house,'' she answered with a dark look. "And so are the lessons in child care."

He put the bill back into his wallet.

"There's a lot more to taking care of a baby than you might realize, Mr. Harrison. Maybe you ought to consider taking your daughter back to her mother."

Sam froze. "No way is my daughter going to be an unwanted child! Her mother put her in my SUV without my knowledge. As far as I'm concerned, that means Annie is mine. I love her, and I'm not giving her back."

Laura's opinion of him went up another notch. A man who loved children had to be a decent man. Only, not the man for her.

She remembered all too well the early years of her own life when, as an unwanted child, she'd been shuffled from foster home to foster home. Until she was twelve, and Elsie and Jonah Evans had appeared out of nowhere to adopt her. She'd been grateful, had come to love them dearly and had cared for them until they'd passed on. Little Annie was lucky. She might have a mother who didn't want her, but she had a father who adored her.

"As for my learning how to take care of my daughter," Sam continued, "I'm game. That is, if you're still willing to teach me what I need to know."

Willing to take care of Annie when I fell in love with her the moment she smiled at me? You bet!

But how was she going to handle Annie's father?

A glance at miniscule lips sucking a tiny hand settled the problem. At least for the moment, Laura thought, grateful for the diversion. "Now that Annie's comfortable, it's time to feed her."

When Sam looked lost, she rummaged through the baby's diaper bag. "Any formula in here, or was the baby being breast-fed?"

He shook his head. "Knowing Paige, I doubt it. She wasn't around that much between flights. Actually her mother helped take care of the baby. As for any formula being in the bag, I haven't the foggiest notion. I didn't have time to look before you came to our rescue. Which reminds me," he went on, "I forgot to thank you for taking us in."

Laura sat back on her heels and regarded Sam with a raised eyebrow. "Just how old is Annie? I need to know so I can take care of her properly."

"Five, maybe six months."

"You're not sure?"

He tried to look innocent and felt defensive at the same time. "I was on assignment when she was born. Okay, okay," he added when she continued to stare at him in disbelief, "I'd say maybe six months."

Laura went back to rummaging in the diaper bag.

"There has to be baby cereal around here some-place, unless Annie's not eating solids yet."

"Sorry, I'm afraid I don't know that, either."

He looked so lost Laura decided maybe she'd been too hard on him. "Not to worry. From Annie's healthy appearance, I'd say someone took good care of her."

She gathered Annie in her arms, nestled her against her chest and brushed the baby's velvet cheek with her lips. Murmuring softly, she grabbed the diaper bag and gestured to Sam's duffel. "Maybe you'd like to get cleaned up while I take Annie into the kitchen and find out just what we do have in here."

"I'd be mighty grateful to get out of these wet clothes." He gestured to his wet shirt and soaking jeans, and shrugged helplessly.

Laura's gaze focused on a shirt so wet it was transparent. Under it, wide shoulders, a muscular chest and dark-brown curls were as visible as in an artist's rendition. She didn't dare look below his waist.

"No problem," she said nonchalantly. "Go on upstairs and take the first room on the right. If you don't have everything you need in your duffel bag, check the closet."

Sam halted in midstride. "You're married?"

"No," Laura answered. "The clothing belonged

to my dad. I've never gotten around to packing it up and giving it away.''

Sam muttered his thanks and fled temptation as quickly as his bare feet would take him. The sight of Annie in the ranch owner's arms hit him where it hurt. Turned his thoughts to early dreams of a warmhearted wife and children of his own. Before his world caved in on him.

The look in Laura's eyes reminded him he was on probation as a father. Maybe as a man, too.

Considering the situation, he might be better off out of sight. At least until he'd cleaned up, rescued his boots and was able to take charge again.

The bedroom she'd directed him to appeared to be some kind of dormitory. A kid's dormitory, judging from the size of the trio of bunk beds and the rest of the furniture. Footlockers under the beds took the place of dressers. One small chest of drawers was in a corner with a brass lamp on it. The beds were covered with handmade quilts, freshly starched green-and-white curtains hung on the windows, and a large hooked rug covered the floor. From the look of the room, Laura must be expecting the campers she'd mentioned.

The child-size bunk beds were definitely not intended for a six-foot-two-inch man. Unless he curled into a pretzel shape and let his legs hang over the edge. A bunk might be okay for Annie, if she didn't turn over and topple off.

Between the too-short bunk bed and worrying about Annie, how in hell was he going to get any sleep tonight?

Through an open door, he caught a glimpse of a bathroom. Good, he thought as he shucked his damp clothing down to his shivering skin. A long hot shower was just the ticket. Cleaned up and with his boots on, he could face the lady rancher on equal terms.

In the bathroom an old-fashioned claw-foot tub greeted him. The sink was of the same vintage, maybe thirty years old or more. The shower was over the tub and enclosed by a plastic shower curtain. At least the tub was man-size, Sam mused gratefully as he stepped into the tub and let hot water run over him.

To his surprise, he found his boots, cleaned and shined, just inside the door when he came back into the bedroom. Room service? He let out a sigh of relief. Maybe his stay at the ranch was going to be more enjoyable than he'd thought.

He rummaged in his duffel for clean jeans and a fresh shirt. Once dressed, he took the stairs two at a time and headed for the sounds coming from the kitchen.

Annie was sitting on a stack of pillows. A large

kitchen towel around her middle bound her firmly to the rungs of a kitchen chair. Her little hands were waving in the air, and milk dripped from her chin. Laura was laughing and waving a spoon to catch the baby's attention. Sure enough, an enchanted Annie's lips parted.

One swoop, another, then *plop,* the cereal went into Annie's open mouth. Beside them, the alert mutt stood with his tongue hanging out, his tail wagging. From the expectant look in his eyes, Sam expected kindhearted Laura to give the dog his turn.

Sam stood silently, lost in thought. He'd usually been on the outside of life, photographing heartwarming scenes for others to enjoy. This one, with his own daughter in it, warmed his heart. Too bad his ex hadn't hung around long enough to be a part of a scene like this.

Sam had thought he'd realized his dream of having a family of his own. Until Paige had told him he wasn't a good husband, let alone father. Annie had been a mistake, she'd explained when she'd called him from Paris and told him she'd filed for divorce.

He gazed at little Annie. With her golden-brown hair, chocolate-brown eyes and a dimple in her chin, she was almost a mirror image of himself.

Annie, a mistake? No way. Annie was the best thing that had ever happened to him. She might have a mother who'd opted out of motherhood, but she sure had a father who wanted her.

The domestic scene in front of him was unsettling. He told himself he still had mountains to climb, roads to travel, photographs to take. That it was the wrong time and place to become maudlin over broken dreams.

He'd have to forget the attraction he was beginning to feel for Laura, both for her sake and for his. His first priority was to prove he could make it as a father—or bust a gut trying.

Laura Evans apparently had problems of her own, anyway. She didn't need him to complicate her life.

There was only one thing left to do, he thought as he cleared his throat and made his presence known. As soon as the car-rental agency turned up with another vehicle, he'd take Annie, do Laura a favor and get out of her life.

Arm in midair, Laura looked up at Sam. In a clean, although wrinkled, white shirt and fresh khakis, he looked taller, more sure of himself. Maybe not as sexy as he'd looked when he was dripping wet, but definitely interesting.

"Hungry?" she asked. Annie banged her spoon on the table and babbled a welcome. The dog growled at the interruption.

"Sure," Sam answered with a grin. "That is, if

you have something more filling than baby cereal around."

"Of course," Laura answered. "Just give me a minute to finish feeding Annie."

"How about letting me take over?" Sam suggested. "I may as well learn the drill."

Laura regarded him thoughtfully before she stood and handed him the spoon. "Of course. Just don't put too much on the spoon at one time or she'll choke."

Sam sensed her reluctance. He understood her dilemma all too well. He might be Annie's father, but Laura was concerned he might not be able to do the right thing for the baby. "With you here to supervise, I'll do fine," he said bravely. "Just wait and see."

"I wasn't expecting company," Laura answered. "Ham and eggs and hash browns for supper okay with you?"

Sam sat down and gingerly dipped the spoon into the cereal and aimed for Annie's mouth. "Sure," he answered. Happily Annie was hungry enough to cooperate. "By the way, thanks for cleaning my boots."

"It wasn't me," Laura answered as she rummaged in an old refrigerator. "Hank took care of it. Said a man without his boots is like a fish out of water."

"My thoughts exactly," Sam answered, wiping excess cereal off Annie's chin. "Who's Hank? I'd like to thank him."

"The ranch handyman," Laura answered. "He's been around here for more years than he can remember. Not that there's a lot for him to do anymore," she added as she sliced a shank of ham, "but he said that since the old sheep herder's life has passed him by, he might as well hang around here."

Sam nodded. From their surroundings, he sensed Hank remained at the ranch because he cared for the place and its present owner. It wasn't difficult to understand, Sam thought as he watched Laura break eggs into a buttered frying pan. Judging from the way she took to caring for Annie, she was the nurturing type. And the nurturing didn't stop with babies.

Laura slid a plate with scrambled eggs, ham and hash browns toward Sam. "Toast and coffee will be ready in a minute."

Sam studied his daughter. She'd spit out the last two spoonfuls of cereal and was hanging over the towel babbling at the mutt. Sam heaved a sigh of relief. Annie was obviously full.

Laura joined him at the table with a plate of her own. "Room okay?"

"Sort of," he answered, debating the wisdom of complaining about the size of the bunk beds. "But to tell you the truth, I'm a little worried about where Annie is going to sleep.''

Laura jumped up to turn off the coffeepot before it boiled over. ''Not to worry,'' she answered as she buttered wheat toast and placed it on a plate. ''There's always the dresser drawer.''

Sam felt himself blanch. ''The dresser? How is she going to breathe in there?''

Laura smiled reassuringly and poured coffee. ''You don't have to worry. We'll improvise. If you're going to be traveling around with Annie, you're going to have to find ways to make do, starting now. Although,'' she added with a frown, ''I don't think traveling with an infant as young as Annie is a good idea.''

Sam shrugged. ''Don't have a choice. At least, not for now. I'll try to find a more permanent place to stay later. Somewhere I can bring in a nanny while I work.''

Laura leaned over to make sure Annie was still securely fastened to the chair. ''Sounds to me it's not going to be easy.'' She bit her lip, reached for her cup of coffee and met Sam's gaze. ''It's okay to leave her here while you do your thing at the spa. That is, if you feel okay leaving her here with me.''

Sam was agreeable to leaving Annie here all right, but only as long as the photography assignment would take. ''I'm game if you don't mind,'' he finally answered. "It'll only take me a couple of days of shooting at the spa, and I'll be back here at night."

Laura was torn between offering him her ancient truck to get to the spa or withholding the offer to keep him from leaving. Until she noticed Annie's drooping eyelids.

"Let's go upstairs, and I'll show you where Annie can spend the night."

"Maybe I can help you clean up in here?"

"Later," Laura answered. She untied the sleepy baby and cuddled her in her arms. "Let's get Annie to bed first. The dishes can wait."

Sam carried the diaper bag and trailed Laura up the stairs. Something told him the next lesson was going to be a zinger.

It was. After Laura cleaned up the sleepy baby, she rummaged in the diaper bag for nightclothes and came up with a yellow fleece sleepsuit. "Looks as if her mother thought of everything Annie would need for today at least," she murmured. "Any more of the baby's things in the SUV?"

"Don't know. Frankly I didn't take time to look around. All I could think of was getting Annie out of there before the deluge hit her."

Laura nodded. "Good thinking. Now, why don't you pull out the bottom drawer of that chest over there and I'll make Annie's bed."

Puzzled, Sam pulled out the empty drawer, brought it over to the bunk bed and watched Laura stuff the drawer with linens. In minutes she had a sleeping Annie tucked into the drawer on her back. ''Annie will be safe in here.''

Sam was lost in admiration at the makeshift crib.

He spent the rest of the evening and the night waiting for Annie to cry. And hoping that Laura wouldn't come barreling in to rescue her. The last thing he wanted was to see Laura in a nightgown. He might have sworn off women for now, but he wasn't a saint.

Chapter Three

In the morning Sam had just polished off the last bit of French toast when he heard a car drive up to the back door of the house, skid to a stop, and a car door slam. To his surprise, Laura glanced out the window and reached for the rifle that hung on a wall.

"Hold on a minute!" Sam jumped to his feet and made for the door. "Take it easy before that thing goes off and you shoot someone."

"You got it right, Sam. That's the idea here." Laura tried to stare him down. "Now get out of my way before the someone turns out to be you."

Sam swallowed hard and took a firm grip of Laura's shooting arm. With Annie asleep in a nest of blankets in the next room, he wasn't about to let the rifle go off. "Not before you tell me what's going on."

"I intend to run an unwanted rat off my property, that's what," she answered with a hot glance over

Sam's shoulder. "Remove your hand and get out of the way."

Sam froze. If it was going to be a question of who was the stronger of the two, he was—hands down. Even though the fire in Laura's eyes told him she wasn't going to give up easily, he didn't intend to move.

A hard impatient knock sounded at the door.

Sam took a firmer grip on the rifle. "At least tell me who's out there, what they want, and why you want to shoot him!"

"Harry Magraw, that's who. And my land, that's what," she answered with a tug on the rifle. "This isn't the first time Magraw has been here uninvited trying to persuade me to sell the ranch. I told him never to show up at the front door again, so this time he's come around to the back door. The fool just doesn't seem to understand the word *no*."

Sam recalled his first impression of the ranch— bare land, a few sheep and no sign of any real activity. The ranch didn't appear productive, let alone valuable. A losing proposition, sure, although he hadn't noticed a FOR SALE sign. "Buy your ranch? Why, is it for sale?"

"No, it's not," she answered. "Even if it were, the last person I would sell it to was someone who wants to turn it into a waste-dump site! My folks loved this ranch, every inch of it, and so do I. Now let go!''

"Okay, but promise me you won't shoot anyone." At her reluctant nod, Sam let go of her arm. "Go ahead, open the door. I'll be right behind you in case there's a problem."

Laura snorted. "Nothing I can't handle." She flung the door open and stepped out onto the porch.

When he spotted Laura's rifle, the short rotund man dressed in an ill-fitting white linen suit took a step backward. "Now see here, Ms. Evans, take it easy. I came here to up my previous offer. No need for a weapon."

Laura glowered at Magraw. "I told you before my ranch isn't for sale. Not under any circumstances, and especially not to you. What part of *no* don't you understand?"

Magraw held up a pudgy hand. "Now see here, Ms. Evans. You and I know you don't have the money to hire hands to maintain this property, even if you do manage to hold on to it. You can't take care of the livestock, either."

Laura shifted the rifle. "I'm warning you. Get off my property!"

Magraw eyed the rifle warily but held his ground. "Do yourself a favor and accept my client's latest offer. With that kind of money, you'd be able to go off and live like a queen anywhere you like."

Laura snorted. "My finances are none of your business, Mr. Magraw. As for living like a queen, I'm doing it right here without your help. You're trespassing. I'm warning you for the last time, get off my property, and don't come back!"

To Sam's surprise, Magraw kept talking. "From what I hear, you're going to lose the property one way or another. Think about it. If you don't accept my client's offer, you won't come out of this with a cent to call your own."

Before Laura could raise the rifle, Sam stepped in front of her. "You heard Ms. Evans. Why don't you leave before someone gets hurt?"

"Who are you?" Magraw demanded with a scowl. "Ain't seen you around these parts."

"No one you need to know," Sam answered. He reached behind him, grasped the handle of the rifle praying it wouldn't go off and shoot him in the foot. Just to make sure, he held the muzzle away from him. "Now, do yourself a favor and leave quietly."

Magraw thrust out his jaw. "Seems to me you don't have a say in what happens to the ranch. Un-less—" he smirked "—you and the lady are some kind of kissin' kin."

Laura gasped and tried to push her way in front of Sam. Out of the corner of his eye, Sam saw Hank coming around the house and starting for the porch. Sam caught his eye and shook his head. The last thing he wanted was an all-out free-for-all, let alone a shooting. He wasn't that anxious to die. "I think you've said enough. Get out of here. Now!"

When Magraw hesitated, Sam shifted the rifle and raised a questioning eyebrow. With a final look at the weapon, Magraw cursed and took off for his car.

Sam waited until the car disappeared down the road before he waved off Hank, turned and led the way into the kitchen.

"Somehow I don't think you've seen the last of Magraw." Sam gingerly put the gun down on the table, stood back and eyed it warily. "Sounds to me as if someone wants to get their hands on your ranch pretty bad. I don't think they'll stop with Magraw."

Laura stomped her way into the kitchen. "I can take care of them, too."

Sam shuddered at the thought of Laura defending her territory with the rifle. "Maybe, maybe not. Now unload that damn thing and put it back where it came from."

"It's not loaded," Laura said with an icy look. "You didn't think I'd keep a loaded rifle around, did you? It's not safe."

"You could have fooled me," Sam answered with an anxious glance at the rifle. "Loaded or not, get rid of it, please."

Laura picked up the gun and stored it in the

broom closet. "You act as if you've never handled a weapon before."

Sam reached for his cold cup of coffee, took a deep swallow and grimaced. "Never before, and never again," he said fervently. He strode to the door leading to the living room to check on Annie. The baby was fast asleep on a nest of blankets on the floor. The dog lay stretched out beside her, his nose between his paws, his unblinking eyes watching Sam.

Sam muttered a prayer of thanks at the way Laura's pet had bonded with the baby. He turned back to the kitchen and to Laura. "Now please sit down and give me the details while my heart slows down to normal."

"What details?"

The way Laura asked the question told Sam she thought it was none of his business. Except now that he'd seen the lengths Laura intended to go, he was making it his business. "Magraw said you're on the verge of losing the ranch. True?"

Normally a private person used to taking care of herself, Laura considered the question. Sam Harrison may be a man she'd only met yesterday, yet there was something about him that made her feel she could trust him.

"Here, let me warm that coffee for you. But first have some of this." Laura reached into the refrigerator, took out the remains of a chocolate cake and set it on the table. "Hank tells me chocolate cake always gives him a shot in the arm. You look like you need it."

Sam regarded the three-tiered chocolate cake and enviously thought of the way the old ranch hand must enjoy Laura's tender loving care. "You bake cakes for the help?"

"Hank's more than help," she said simply. "He's family."

Sam was ready to believe it. From the way she'd taken to Annie, it was too bad she didn't have children of her own. He owed her. "Anything I can do around here while I wait for the replacement car?"

"No, thanks." She poured Sam a fresh cup of black coffee and another for herself. "I'm used to making do on my own."

Sam glanced at the broom closet. "Without the gun, I hope. So, how about telling me what the problem is. Money?"

Laura shrugged helplessly. "Magraw was right. I don't have enough funds to increase the herd or to hire men to take care of the small amount of stock I do have. Hank does the best he can, but that's not the only problem. There's…" Her voice trailed off as she moved to gaze out the window.

Sam rose and went to stand beside her. The sadness in her voice, the anxious look in her eyes troubled him. As far as he could tell, she was alone in the fight to keep her heritage.

He knew from being alone. It was a cold place no one, especially a caring woman like Laura, should have to experience. She needed a sympathetic ear, and he was ready and willing to listen. It was the least he could do for her in exchange for all she'd done for Annie and for him. "There's what?"

"Taxes," she said succinctly. "I'm about to open a camp for young children in order to make enough money to pay the next installment, due next month."

Sam nodded. "Do you really think boarding six kids for the summer is going to be enough to keep the ranch going?"

"It's a start. If all goes well, we'll advertise for more campers."

"Who's we?"

"Katy O'Donnell. Katy's been a friend of mine since we worked at the hospital. She's planning on coming here to help out."

Now Sam was really interested. Instead of the camp being a pipe dream, the idea was sounding better by the minute. "Another nurse?" Laura nodded. "Seems to me you're right. The camp is a good place to start. Are you sure there's nothing I can do to help?"

Laura shook her head. "No, thanks. You have

your own life to take care of. I need to take care of mine. Not that I don't appreciate your offer,'' she hurried to add, ''but this is something I have to do myself.''

Sam glanced out the window to where Hank was entering the barn. ''How does Hank enter the picture?''

''Like I said, he's family.''

Lucky Hank. Lucky Annie. Lucky him, Sam mused. Lucky to have found a woman as strong and big-hearted as Laura Evans. After the way he'd trashed her ranch, any other woman would have sent him packing. ''Where are you going to find the campers?''

''I advertised in a parents magazine. So far I have five positive replies and one maybe.''

''Are five kids enough to make the difference?''

''Not really,'' she replied with a wry smile. ''I'm taking one day at a time.''

Sam looked back at the chocolate cake. ''If word gets out about what a great cook you are, you'll probably have more campers than you can handle.''

''I wish.'' She laughed. ''Are ham and eggs and chocolate cake enough to impress you?''

''You bet. Some people, myself included, can't boil water.'' He went back, sat down at the kitchen table and dug into the cake. ''You can cook for me anytime.''

She laughed again and cut him another piece of cake.

Sam liked the sound of Laura's laugh. He liked a lot more about her, too, and not only her cooking. The way a dimple danced across her cheek when she smiled. The way she smiled at him. Her open heart, her courage when faced with a situation that would have sent most women running.

Laura felt herself blush when she saw admiration shining in Sam's eyes. It was a good thing he was leaving in a few days, she thought. She couldn't take being around him without thinking the impossible. Sam and his infant daughter reminded her of her dream of a family of her own. An unlikely dream at best.

She was saved from her thoughts by a knock on the front door.

"Laura? Laura, are you in there?"

Relieved, Laura made for the front door with Sam hard on her heels. "It's Pete Dolan, the county sheriff," she said over her shoulder, and opened the door. "Hi, Pete. Come on in. What's up?"

Pete opened the screen door, came into the living room and eyed Sam. "Heard you had company."

"News travels fast around here, but not that fast." Her eyes narrowed. "Who have you been talking to—Magraw?"

"Yep. He stopped in the office and told me your friend here threatened him with a rifle."

"*I* was the one who threatened him with the rifle, but it wasn't loaded," she answered heatedly. "I don't even own any ammunition. It was dad's old hunting rifle, and you know full well it's not operable."

Pete raised an eyebrow. "So your friend here had nothing to do with the confrontation?"

"Not really," she said. "Well, maybe. If Magraw wasn't such a jerk, he'd have noticed that when Sam took hold of the gun, he had the muzzle pointed at the floor."

Sam stepped forward and held out his hand. "The name's Sam Harrison. I'm not exactly a friend of Ms. Evans's. The truth is, I ran off the road yesterday and banged up my car."

Pete nodded as he shook Sam's hand. "Noticed the busted fence and the remains of the water tower as I drove in. You responsible?"

"Sorry to say, I am." Sam managed a grin, but he wasn't too happy about the grim look on the sheriff's face. With the accident and the rifle business, he sensed he already had two strikes against him. It wouldn't take much to reach three. "Ms. Evans was kind enough to offer me a place to stay until the rental agency in Grand Junction sends down a replacement vehicle. Seems there's a holiday getting in the way.''

Annie began to cry.

Dolan looked over at the baby and back at Sam. ''Yours?''

''Mine.'' Sam strode over to pick up the baby, then held her to his shoulder and patted her on her back to comfort her. The mutt took a stand at his feet.

''Is there a Mrs. Harrison around here?''

Sam shook his head. ''The ex-Mrs. Harrison is somewhere over the skies of France. Annie and I are on our own.''

Laura stepped into the conversation. ''Come on, Pete. Magraw was out of line by coming back here after I'd already ordered him off the property, and you know it. Sam was only trying to help me get rid of the jerk.''

Dolan regarded Sam with a calculating look. ''Got any identification? Driver's license? Car-rental agreement?''

Sam handed Annie to Laura, dug into his back pocket and took out his wallet. Under the sheriff's watchful gaze, he handed over his worn driver's license.

''Move around a lot, do you?''

Sam took out his business card and car-rental agreement and handed them to Dolan. ''I'm a photojournalist. It's a profession that keeps me on the move.''

"Don't own a car?''

"No. Like you said, I move around a lot. It's actually cheaper for me to rent a car than to own one.''

Dolan studied the license, the business card and the auto-rental agreement long enough to raise the hair on the back of Sam's neck. When Dolan handed back the papers, the look in his eyes told Sam he wasn't welcome around here.

"How long did you say you intended to stick around?''

"I didn't.'' The narrowing of the sheriff's eyes told Sam his instincts had been right. Dolan wasn't too happy to have him here, let alone staying in the same house as Laura. "Until the rental agency gets me a replacement vehicle,'' Sam repeated. "Maybe a few days, a week, tops.''

The sheriff nodded, but to Sam's discomfiture, didn't smile before he spoke to Laura. "I'll talk to Magraw and see to it he gets the message he's not wanted around here. Do yourself a favor, Laura. Put the rifle away and don't bring it out again.'' He started out the door, then glanced over his shoulder at Sam. "I'll be back later.''

Sam let out his breath when the door closed behind Dolan. "Somehow that sounds like a threat, not a promise. I don't blame the sheriff, though. Magraw must have really filled his ear."

"Pete's an old friend of my father's. He drops in regularly to check on me," Laura explained with a weak grin. "I guess I'd better put the rifle in the barn. I'll be back in a minute."

Sam watched her go. He wasn't happy about Dolan's attitude, but at least someone was going to keep an eye on Laura after his car arrived and he moved on.

He watched Laura head across the yard and disappear into the barn. She was an interesting mix, he mused admiringly. Brave, hot-tempered, and yet there was something vulnerable about her. How could he think of walking away from her without trying to help?

He parked himself on the couch and propped a drooling Annie on his knees. "Between you and me, sweetheart, maybe I should have my head examined, but I'm thinking of getting involved here. What do you say?"

Annie smiled, blew a drool bubble and waved her arms. The mutt, who'd obviously decided Annie belonged to him, barked. Sam took these as signs of approval.

"Glad you both feel that way," Sam went on. "I intended to move on as soon as I got a replacement car, but something tells me Laura could use another friend.''

Annie bobbed her head and reached for Sam's nose. "Right," he said, grabbing her little hand in his and rubbing it against his cheek. "So this is my game plan, guys. I'm going to tell Laura I need to stick around long enough to take a few more lessons on the care and feeding of infants. Seeing how she takes to you, sweetheart, I figure I have it made."

"Got what made?" Laura stood in the doorway with Hank at her back.

Sam felt like a fool, but the damage was done. He thought fast. "It looks as if Annie's running out of diapers, so I figured I'd ask you for a lift into town to buy fresh supplies. You do have some sort of vehicle around here, don't you?"

Laura looked doubtful, probably because his explanation didn't compute with what she'd overheard.

Lucky for him, Laura smiled her agreement. If all he needed was to draw Annie into the equation to make Laura smile, he was home free.

"That's a good idea," Laura answered. "I've made a list of a few items Annie will need. It's in the kitchen. Here, let me take Annie while you meet Hank."

"Hank Dooley's the name." The elderly man thrust out his hand. "Wanted to thank you for sticking up for Laura back there."

"My pleasure." Sam's hand was swallowed by Hank's. "I didn't want to see Laura get hurt. Or," he added with a wry grin, "hurt someone else."

"Nah, that old rifle ain't worth a damn. Hasn't been shot for years. Laura keeps it to remind her of Jonah, or I'd get rid of it."

"Jonah?"

"Her late father." Hank cocked his head. "Maybe I ought to let Laura tell you about him and Elsie. Nice kid you've got there," he added. "Well, got to go and start putting that fence back together."

"Need any help?"

"No thanks," Hank said with a grin and a pointed glance at Sam's callus-free hands. "If you don't mind my saying so, I don't think you're the guy to do it."

Sam sensed there was a story behind Jonah and Elsie, but thought it best to let Laura tell it herself. From the sound of Hank's voice, it wasn't going to be an ordinary story, either. But then, neither was his.

"Here you are." Laura handed Sam the list. "This ought to hold you for a few days. At least until you get to where you're going."

Sam felt guilty. As far as he was concerned, he *was* where he intended to be, at least for now. It was just a matter of convincing Laura.

Laura handed Annie back when Laura's telephone

rang. "You're a regular bouncing ball, aren't you, pumpkin?" Sam said to the baby. "Good thing you're so good-natured about it."

It was true, thank God. Considering the events of the past two days, it was a miracle the only things that seemed to bother Annie were wet diapers and an empty stomach. Changes in her surroundings and people seemed to fascinate her. Even the mutt, back to parking himself at Sam's feet, didn't scare the baby. She was one tough little cookie.

"Great!" Laura said happily in the background. "Come on over—I've been waiting for you! That was Katy," she explained as she hung up. "You know, the friend who's going to help me get the camp started. Pete's bringing her over."

Sam was pleased with the news about Katy. But not about Dolan coming back so soon to muddy the waters. From the way the ranch looked, Laura needed all the friends she could find. Even though she didn't know it yet, that included him.

Chapter Four

To Sam's disgust, Dolan kept his promise and showed up again that afternoon. At least this time he brought good news with him.

"Katy!" Laura rushed down the steps and threw her arms around the woman who emerged from Dolan's black-and-white official car carrying an overnight bag. "I'm so happy you could make it. How long can you stay?"

"As if anything could keep me away." Katy laughed, returning the hug. "I quit the hospital job, and I'm here to stay, honey, if you want me. The rest of my luggage is coming later."

"Wonderful!" Laura grabbed the overnight bag and drew Katy into the house. "Come on inside. I want you to meet someone. You, too, Pete," she called over Katy's shoulder when the sheriff hesitated.

Inside the house Katy eyed Sam and Annie with

a broad smile. "A prospective camper? I didn't know we were going to take them so young."

"Not really," Laura replied. "Sam, this is the friend I told you about, Katy O'Donnell. Katy, this is Sam Harrison. He and Annie are staying with us for a few days."

Sam tucked Annie under his arm and rose to meet the dark-haired woman, a friendly smile on his face. From the shrewd look in her eyes as she sized him up, it was clear she was a no-nonsense kind of a woman. Good, he thought. If anyone would be able to help keep Laura's ranch on an even course to solvency, it would be someone like Katy.

"Pleased to meet you," he answered. "You might say Annie and I are kind of visiting."

"Kind of?"

"Yes. I'm the guy who took down the fence." He chuckled ruefully. "Worse yet, I took down the water tower and trashed my SUV in the process. Lucky for me Laura is the forgiving type. She's letting me hang around until I get a few things straightened out."

Across the room, Sam saw the sheriff staring at him. The look on the sheriff's face told Sam the sheriff wasn't inclined to be as forgiving as Laura. Maybe because the guy knew the broken fence and the loss of the water tower was damned inconvenient for a rancher, let alone how much it would cost to restore.

"Brought you your mail, Laura." Dolan handed over a small stack of envelopes. "Hope it's what you've been waiting for."

With a squeal of delight, Laura leafed through the small stack of envelopes. "It looks as if these are applications for the camp."

"How many?" Katy took off her jacket, sat down on the couch and took off her shoes.

"Five applications!" Laura said gleefully. "And one maybe."

Sam felt like cheering.

"By the way, Laura," the sheriff began ominously, "I've been a friend of yours from the time you were a little squirt, so I can talk to you. I'd hate to see anything bad happen to you."

Laura's smile disappeared. Her face turned white. "What's wrong? What do you mean by 'bad'?"

Dolan looked uncomfortable, even reluctant, before he finally answered. "I thought you should know Magraw hasn't given up. When I got back to the office, I found him waiting for me and mighty anxious to shoot off his mouth again."

"What about?"

Dolan looked at Sam. "I'd rather not say right now."

"From the look on your face," Sam broke in, the

hair on the back of his neck quivering, "I get the feeling the bad news concerns me. Why don't you just spit it out?"

The sheriff hesitated. Sam mentally reviewed his bank account, but he didn't think that was the problem. Since Hank had sounded as if he had the fence repair taken care of, maybe he didn't have to worry about paying for a new one. As for the water tower, as soon as he was paid for his photo shoot at the spa, he just might squeeze out enough money to replace it.

"Pete!" Laura prodded. "What did Magraw say?"

As if he could read Sam's thoughts, Dolan glanced over at him grimly. "Like I said, maybe it would be better if we had this conversation in private."

Laura's gaze met Sam's in time to see a shadow pass over his face. Of course he could stay. He was a strong, yet gentle man who had stood up for her and deserved her respect.

She was also highly attracted to him. It wouldn't have taken much encouragement for her to think of Sam as more than a friend. Maybe in another lifetime, she thought sadly. Right now, friendship was good. She didn't think she could handle any more complications in her life.

"That's not necessary, Pete," she said quietly.

"Mr. Harrison has earned the right to listen to what you have to say. Go ahead."

Katy spoke up when Dolan continued to hesitate. "I don't know what went on around here with this fellow Magraw, but if Laura is willing to let Mr. Harrison stay, that ought to be good enough for you."

Clearly embarrassed, Dolan ran his fingers through his hair, shuffled his feet and looked over Laura's head. "Don't know how to tell you this without sounding out of line, Laura, but Magraw as good as said you and Harrison look like you're living together."

Laura gasped. "So that's what he meant by 'kissin' kin.' That's ridiculous! He's just trying to get even with me because Sam ran him off."

"Maybe," Pete replied with another disapproving glance at Sam, "but you know what people are going to think if Magraw keeps shooting off his mouth about Harrison threatening him with a rifle. As for Harrison living here, well, that's your business." He flushed and cleared his throat. "You ought to remember it ain't going to help your reputation."

"My reputation's just fine, thank you," Laura retorted. "In the first place, Sam and I aren't alone. Hank's here. In the second place, even if we are, it's none of Magraw's business."

"Maybe so," Pete said stubbornly. "But you

have to think about that kids' camp you want to start. We're a small community here, and you know as well as I do gossip spreads like wildfire. If this gets around, you might not have any takers for your camp."

Laura looked shaken and glanced uneasily at Sam. "Pete may be right about that. I have to make the camp a success in order to keep the ranch."

Now that the other shoe had dropped, Sam let out his breath. "If it will help, I'll take Annie and leave tonight."

Katy got to her feet. "No, wait a minute, everyone! If people around here listen to any gossip that man Magraw spreads, then they don't know our Laura. Besides, now that I'm here to stay, no one's going to talk about who lives here." She stared at Sam as if daring him to object. "Now give me that baby, Mr. Harrison. I'm not going to rest until I get my hands on the little darling."

"You and everyone else," Sam agreed with a wry smile. "Better warn you, she needs a diaper change."

"No problem. I'm a pro." Katy cuddled Annie in her arms and tickled the baby's ribs. "We're going to get along just fine, aren't we, dumpling?" Annie burbled her agreement. Katy laughed when the baby reached for her hair. "By the way, Laura," she went on. "I'm starved. How about some lunch? That bagel and coffee I had for breakfast didn't cut it."

"Of course," Laura agreed with a faint smile. "Now that you've gotten the bad news off your chest, Pete, we can forget it." She went to the door. "Come on in, Hank. I'm making sandwiches for everyone."

Sam realized Laura was trying to put a cheerful face on the situation, but he knew better. Her smile may have been for Katy's sake, but the look in her eyes told the true story. She was deeply troubled, and he was partially to blame. What to do about it was the problem.

Katy rummaged in the diaper bag on the floor by the fireplace, fished out a bottle while she sized up Annie's father. "Why don't you let Mr. Harrison help you, Laura? Two hands are better than one."

Sam was taken by surprise, until he realized Katy wanted to get rid of him. "Sure, I'll be glad to help," he said. He kissed Annie on the cheek. "I'll be back soon, sweetheart."

Katy waited until the door closed behind Sam. "Now see here, Mr. Dolan…"

The sheriff eyed the closed kitchen door with concern before he pulled his attention back to Katy. "If you're going to stay around here, you may as well call me Pete."

"Sure, whatever," Katy said as she changed the

baby's diaper. "Like I started to say, I haven't seen Laura as glowing as she is today, unless it was the time the quints were born at the hospital three years ago. Something tells me it isn't my arrival that's doing it, either."

Dolan scratched his chin. "Maybe you're right. Laura *has* been kind of quiet lately. I figured it was her financial problems."

"Maybe so," Katy said. "Then again, maybe not. Laura's a sensible self-sufficient kind of woman, but she still needs to have someone she cares for to talk to. The way I see it, that someone is Sam Harrison."

Dolan snorted. "Sounds to me more like he's a here-today-gone-tomorrow sort of fellow, or he wouldn't be roaming around without a wife and a baby as young as that one. It ain't right."

"A man who takes on a baby to care for isn't the irresponsible kind, Pete. I don't know why he showed up here, but I'm sure that when Laura's ready, she'll tell me the story. So why don't you stand aside and let nature take its course?"

Dolan appealed to Hank for help. "Just like a woman, ain't it? Hardly one foot in the door and already matchmaking!"

Hank shrugged and eyed Katy cautiously. "Ain't enough folks around to match."

"You're right." Dolan turned back to Katy. "How do you know a loser like Harrison wants to

get together with Laura? Some men are natural
bachelors—like Hank and me.''

Katy sized him up with a broad grin. ''Oh, I don't
know.'' She chuckled. ''Maybe you're both still single because no woman's set her sights on either of
you before this.''

With an alarmed look at Katy, Hank headed for
the door. ''Count me out, Pete. Oh, and tell Laura
I'll be getting my own grub over at the bunkhouse
from now on.''

LAURA RAIDED the refrigerator and came up with
ham, cheese, lettuce, tomatoes and a jar of mustard.
''I'll have to stock up on more supplies if I'm going
to have campers,'' she murmured. ''How about getting the bread out of the pantry?''

His mind whirling like a broken clock, Sam
headed for the pantry. With Katy here and fathering
lessons probably on hold, he couldn't come up with
a valid reason for hanging around the ranch much
longer. Just as well he'd just about made up his
mind to leave.

Strangely enough, the idea of moving on left him
with an uneasy feeling. What if Laura couldn't pay
the land taxes that were coming due? What if the
bank foreclosed on her? Was he a coward for thinking of running out on her?

In his mind, at least, it came down to this. Dolan

might be Laura's friend, but as sheriff the man had to carry out the law. The more Sam thought about it, the more he realized that what Laura needed was someone who wasn't bound by rules or oaths of office that would keep him from helping her. And unless someone better came along, that someone was him.

"How about some pickles?" he called from the pantry.

"Anything you'd like is fine with me," Laura answered. "Bring it with you."

Anything he liked. What he would have liked was to have some quality time with Laura, Sam thought. Instead, he had an assignment waiting for him and plans to make for Annie's care.

Once lunch was over and the kitchen cleaned up, Laura said to Sam, "Now that Katy's here to keep an eye on Annie, I think I'll go into Montgomery, too. You can pick up a few things for Annie while I order some supplies for the camp."

"I'd appreciate your help," he answered gratefully. "Like I said, what I know about babies wouldn't fit into a thimble."

"Don't worry," Laura laughingly assured him. "By the time you move on, you'll know which end of Annie to diaper and which end to feed. Hang on a minute while I get my things and check with Katy."

Sam trailed Laura into the living room. Katy was curled up on a couch with Annie asleep in her arms. Judging from the look on her face and from the contented look on the sheriff's face—Pete had parked himself in an armchair and was talking to her— Katy's matchmaking had found an unexpected home.

Laura drove her battered pickup as it bumped and swayed along the muddy road leading to Montgomery. When Sam glanced over at her, she appeared deep in thought as the truck ate up the miles to town.

He looked out the window. After Magraw's appearance, his nerves were on edge and his senses heightened. The sky seemed bluer, each blade of grass greener, the clean air sweeter. And as for Laura, although her silken hair was pulled back in a ponytail, tendrils blew around ocean-blue eyes and a mouth that was made to smile.

"Beautiful. Wish I had my camera," he said softly.

Laura murmured her agreement. "The countryside is too beautiful to turn into a dump site, don't you think?"

"You bet," Sam agreed, unable to tell Laura he hadn't been referring to the passing scenery; he'd been referring to her. "Have you lived here all your life?"

"No, mostly in Denver."

"I thought you said the ranch has been in your family for generations."

"Yes. It's only mine because I was adopted when I was twelve. Not that I take the ranch ownership as my right. It's just that I've loved it from the first moment my folks brought me here." She hesitated, then glanced at Sam. "They may be gone now, but even without them I can't let the ranch go."

Sam nodded silently. He knew only too well that sometimes children never felt secure enough to take anything for granted.

His early years flashed through his mind to the time he'd lost his own father. At the time he'd been fifteen. Not a child anymore. With his widowed mother working two jobs and him working one to make ends meet, he hadn't been able to take much in his life for granted. He'd kept his fears and uncertainty about the future to himself.

He'd believed marriage and children would be the answer to feeling wanted and secure. Until Paige's call to tell him she was filing for divorce. He hadn't taken anything for granted since.

The only thing he could believe in and count on was his infant daughter, Annie. She was going to feel loved and secure as long as he had anything to do about it.

The pickup truck suddenly hit a large pothole and slid across the road. "The road needs work," Laura said breathlessly. "Now I understand why you skidded off the road. Under the circumstances, I guess I have to apologize for what I've been thinking about your driving."

"I probably deserved every word of it," Sam answered. He thanked his lucky stars for the seat belt that kept him from sliding into Laura. "I should have been paying more attention to the road. Actually," he added with a wry grin, "I was admiring the scenery." *Just as I am now.*

"I thought you said it was the baby who distracted you."

"Yeah, well, that, too," Sam said. "Finding a baby in the back seat of your car is enough to take years off a man's life. Let alone discovering it's your own kid." He looked out the window. "By the way, you said something about my taking a wrong turn at a fork in the road?"

"We're coming to it now." Laura pointed to a road that ran off at a right angle. "There used to be a sign at the crossroads, but it looks as if the storm the other day took it down. You plan on going over to the spa?"

"Not just yet," he replied. "First things first. I've a few things to settle before I can think of anything else."

Laura bit her lower lip in relief; she'd been so sure Sam was ready to move on. With Annie, Sam had managed to strike the one chord in her that she never failed to respond to. Babies.

She might not be able to have children of her own, but being around infants, even older children, was a joy. "You could leave Annie at my place until you've found a permanent place to live."

Sam looked surprised at her offer. Not that she blamed him. After she'd greeted him at the end of a rifle, how could he be sure of his welcome?

"What with the camp about to start up, I'd say you'd be too busy to care for a baby as young as Annie."

"There's plenty of room," she answered as they approached the hamlet of Montgomery. "Besides, there's Katy to help out now." She pulled up in front of the general store. "Katy would have my hide if you took Annie away before she'd got you trained and straightened out."

"Don't get me wrong," Sam answered. "I'd be grateful if you cared for Annie for a few days while I finish my photo shoot at the spa. But I want to make it clear—I love my daughter and I intend to be the one to raise her."

"Yeah, sure," Laura replied dryly. "As soon as you learn enough to fill that thimble."

Laughing, they entered the general store, where a group of people stood at the counter deep in conversation. Some fell silent when they caught sight of Laura and Sam. Others seemed to avoid meeting Sam's eyes.

The hair on the back of Sam's neck prickled, a sure sign of trouble. Sure as hell, Magraw had been busy spreading the word in town.

He remembered the sheriff's warning. Twenty-first century or not, small towns were different. Newcomers had to prove themselves before they were accepted, and he was no exception. What really bothered him was the way Laura was being treated. She didn't seem to notice the silent treatment, but he did.

"Diapers," Laura announced as she headed for the baby section. "Baby lotion and wipes. Hair shampoo, some cotton shirts, rice cereal, milk and some baby food. I think she has enough bottles, but she'll need teething rings, another baby blanket, talcum powder, a sippy—"

"Hold on a minute," Sam interjected, eyeing the growing pile of baby items with dismay. "I recognize most of those things, but what's a sippy, for heaven's sake?"

"A plastic container with a cup-shaped cover that lets a baby drink without spills," she answered absentmindedly as she fingered soft infant towels. "Which reminds me, Annie will need a few bibs."

"Yeah, sure," Sam answered, although he wasn't sure what a bib was. "Anything else?"

"A lot of love and security," Laura answered as she gathered the items in her arms and led the way to the counter. "Only, they're not for sale. That's where you come in."

"Annie already has them," Sam answered. He reached behind him, picked up a package of pink barrettes and added it to the pile in Laura's arms.

"Barrettes?" Laura looked amused. "Annie doesn't have much hair yet, let alone enough to pull back into a barrette."

"She may not have much hair now, but I'll get these on her somehow," Sam said firmly. "I want everyone to know she's a girl."

Nathan Calhoun, the proprietor of the general store, eyed Sam when they reached the checkout counter. "Heard you were opening a summer camp for little kids, Laura."

"You heard right." Laura reached for a chocolate bar and added it to the stack. "That's for me." She took a small sheet of paper out of her pocket. "That reminds me, Nate. Could you have these items ready for me to pick up next Monday?"

Calhoun glanced at the paper and whistled. "Looks like you're expecting lots of company." He put the list on the cash register and turned his attention to Sam. "You fixin' to be around long?"

Sam reached for his wallet, took out a fifty-dollar

bill and handed it to Calhoun. "Depends. And by the way, I'm paying for the chocolate bar."

Calhoun's eyebrows rose into a vee as he packed the items into large brown bags. "Heard you and Laura are a real twosome."

"Don't believe everything you hear," Sam said quietly. "And especially not the man who tells it to you."

Busy unwrapping the chocolate bar, Laura looked surprised at the interchange. "Have I missed something?"

"Nothing that would interest you," Sam answered as he met the owner's eyes. "Right, Mr. Calhoun?"

The man hesitated, flushed and nodded his head. "If you say so."

"I say so," Sam said quietly. He nodded at Calhoun and led the way out of the store. If he'd doubted his presence at Laura's ranch was harming her reputation, the whispers and sly looks they'd encountered decided it for him.

Damn Magraw and his big mouth to hell and back!

Chapter Five

When the sheriff showed up again the next morning, as far as Sam was concerned, matters didn't look any more promising. To add to his unease, a second car drove up with Magraw and a stranger in it.

Magraw's wrinkled white suit looked as if he'd slept in it. Judging from the dark stubble covering his chin, the guy hadn't even taken the time to shower and shave.

In sharp contrast, the man who accompanied him looked as if he'd stepped off the cover of *Money* magazine. His face was clean-shaven, and his graying hair looked as if it had been styled in a pricey salon.

From the man's tailored navy-blue business suit, pristine white shirt, navy-blue-and-white striped tie and shiny black shoes, Sam sensed the patrician-looking stranger had to be the one who had his eye on Laura's ranch.

It took Sam twenty seconds to make up his mind to get involved. He might only be passing through on his way to God knows where, but he wasn't the kind of man to let Laura go through what would surely be a confrontation alone.

He took a quick mental count of his backup. Including himself, Hank and Katy, there were three people on Laura's side. If he threw in Annie, that made it four to two. The lawman, sworn to do his duty, didn't count.

Sam moved to the top step and motioned for Laura to stand back. Judging from her clenched hands and the grim look on her face, it was obvious she recognized trouble.

Thank God the rifle was safely in the barn.

Magraw opened his mouth to speak. Dolan, beating the guy to the punch, motioned him to silence. "Before we begin, folks, I want you all to know I'm only here to make sure everything stays peaceful." He turned to the stranger. "Go ahead, Mr. Hansen. Speak your piece. Magraw, you just listen."

"Ms. Evans?" the man asked pleasantly. Laura nodded curtly. "My name is Frederick Hansen." He took a business card out of his breast pocket, walked up the steps and held it out to Laura. "I'm the owner of Hansen Waste Management. I'm here because I was sure two reasonable people like us could discuss the sale of your property without outside interference.'' He smiled and paused for effect. When Laura didn't reply, he went on as if she hadn't heard him the first time. ''I'm here to make you an offer for your property.''

''I know what you're here for,'' Laura said. Instead of reaching for the business card, she jammed her hands into her jeans pockets. ''My answer is still the same. Like I told your man Magraw, the ranch isn't for sale.''

Hansen glanced pointedly at Sam, then turned back to Laura. ''Perhaps you've been listening to the wrong advice,'' he said with a smile that didn't reach his eyes. ''If you'll give me a few moments of your time, I'm sure I can persuade you to change your mind.''

After the way Hansen's cool glance dismissed him in passing, Sam was sorry the rifle, broken or not, was in the barn, regardless of the sheriff's presence. The rifle might be useless, but it would have shown Hansen he meant business. Sam gritted his teeth, moved closer to Laura and waited for the man's next move.

''I don't know what kind of advice you're referring to,'' Laura said, ''but this is my property. I don't have to take advice from anyone. My ranch is still not for sale.''

''I wouldn't be too sure about that if I were you, Ms. Evans,'' Hansen persisted. ''If you give me a chance to speak to you privately, I have some information that might make a difference in your decision.''

Sam had had enough. No way was Hansen going to try to intimidate Laura, not while he was here. ''Ms. Evans has just told you she's not interested. Why don't you leave it at that?''

The atmosphere on the porch turned heavy. Dolan cleared his throat, and Hansen lost his smile. ''Are you threatening me, young man?''

Hansen's cold look might have cowed a lesser man, but Sam didn't blink. After photographing spas around the world and taking advantage of their physical-fitness programs, he was ready, willing and able to take the action as far as the guy wanted to go.

''Not at all,'' Sam replied amiably. ''Just making a suggestion you might want to consider.''

In the background, Magraw snorted and pointed at Sam. ''Be careful, Mr. Hansen. That's the guy who had the rifle. Like I told you, he threatened me with it the last time I was here.''

Hansen looked over at Dolan. ''Sheriff, don't just stand there. What are you going to do about this?''

Pete Dolan took the steps two at a time and planted himself in front of Laura. ''Cool down, all of you. Like I said, I'm here to see that no one runs off half-cocked. As for you, Magraw, I told you before that rifle was harmless—it hasn't been used for twenty years. And furthermore, I've taken care of it.'' He waited until Magraw's sputtering subsided. ''And as for you, Mr. Hansen, I'm sure Ms. Evans appreciates your offer, but it's pretty clear she's not interested in selling.''

''Even after she learns the facts?''

Sam's antennae quivered. What had started out as a bad day looked as if it was about to get worse.

Her hands on her hips, Laura pushed the sheriff out of her way. ''What facts?'' she demanded.

''I'd hoped to keep it private,'' Hansen answered, ''but if you're going to insist…I have it on good authority your ranch is about to appear on the delinquent property tax rolls. Once it's published, you'll have thirty days to pay or…'' His voice dripped honey.

''The heck it is!'' Laura glared at Hansen. ''I paid the last two years' taxes myself, and I have the canceled checks to prove it!'' She pointed to the road leading away from the house. ''Now get off my property!''

From the anger on Laura's face, Sam thought she was going to punch Hansen. He sucked in his breath and edged closer to Laura, just in case.

Hansen continued to stand his ground. To add to Sam's unease, Magraw's shouting apparently had been enough to bring Hank out of the barn with the busted rifle in his hand. Sam sucked in his breath and prayed. If this standoff kept up, someone was liable to get hurt.

"Sounds like good advice, Hansen," Sam added when it looked as if Laura had run out of steam. "Why don't you take Magraw and go back where you came from?"

Hansen, his composure visibly rattled at the sight of the gun, managed a smirk. "Maybe Ms. Evans paid up, but her father didn't. Evans apparently ignored county overdue notices for several years before he passed away two years ago. If you ask me, it looks as if the man was too old to know what he was doing." Hansen dropped his business card at Laura's feet. "Call me when you're ready to listen to reason." He turned on his heel, motioned for Magraw to follow him and headed for his car.

The distressed look that crossed Laura's face at Hansen's parting remark damn near broke Sam's heart. Losing her father was bad enough, but to be told the father she'd loved had lost his marbles must really have hurt. Instinctively he put his arm around Laura's shoulders.

He knew all too well how much it meant to have the comfort of personal contact. Especially when your back was to the wall and you felt you were all alone in the world. Maybe he was out of line by holding Laura without a clear invitation, but he couldn't help himself. What he'd really wanted to do was take her in his arms, kiss her frown away and show her he recognized her heartache. Good thing he hadn't gone that far. She would have thought he was a lunatic for sure.

Besides, he'd been down that road before, with disastrous results. With the exception of Annie, of course. Considering the way the baby appeared to have brought him and Laura together, the kid had to be the best thing that had ever happened to him. As for Laura ever falling for him, that was still a question.

He realized he still had his arm around Laura when she looked up at him and blinked. He cleared his throat and removed his arm. "Sorry."

Laura's mind and body warmed at the soft look in Sam's eyes. His strong presence, the warmth of his arm around her shoulders and the concern in his voice made her realize that what she felt for Sam Harrison was more than friendship.

The practical side of her mind told her she was reading more into Sam's embrace than he'd intended. He'd already told her he had plans of his own, hadn't he? She had a children's camp to run and a ranch to hold on to, didn't she?

The dawning comprehension in Pete Dolan's eyes told her he was aware of her reaction to Sam's gesture. She stole a glance at Sam. Was it as obvious to him? And if it was, did he care?

For a moment silence fell. Back in the house, Laura heard Katy offering Annie a bottle. On the porch with her, Sam and Pete Dolan were exchanging thoughtful looks. Over at the barn, Hank disappeared inside, then reemerged without the rifle and headed toward the house. With Katy, Pete, Sam and Hank closing ranks around her, Laura felt blessed.

So why did she still feel so alone?

Pete cleared his throat. "Don't even think about what Hansen said, Laura. If your father paid up, there has to be canceled checks or receipts somewhere. Or if he ignored past due notices, they've got to be around here, too."

"Yes, of course." Laura rubbed a hand across her forehead. "I suppose it's just a matter of knowing where to look. And since I was away at nursing school, then working at the county hospital, I'm not sure where to start looking."

"Better get started soon," Pete answered. "Just keep in mind that tax bills and overdue notices are mailed separately. You're going to have to do some deep checking to make sure you're in the clear." Pete met Sam's eyes.

Sam nodded. He was worldly enough to smell a possible setup when he came across it, and he'd smelled it ever since Hansen and Magraw had arrived on the scene. He took one glance at the lost look in Laura's eyes and added his two cents. "If Laura thinks the back taxes were paid, maybe they were."

"You'll have to have some kind of proof," Pete warned. He shrugged helplessly. "Being the sheriff, I have to stay out of it, or Hansen will think he's getting a bad deal. Just let me know what you come up with."

"Agreed," Sam said. "How about keeping an eye out for Hansen while I try to help Laura?"

To Sam's relief, a look of respect dawned in Dolan's eyes. "I'll do what I can to fend him off," the sheriff answered, "but if Hansen's right, you and Laura have only a few days before things hit the fan."

"Right." Sam looked over at Katy, who appeared at the door carrying Annie. At the sight of her father, the baby gave a wide grin and held out her arms. A burst of love broke over Sam as he reached to take her in his arms. He rubbed noses with her, breathed in her fresh baby scent and realized that being her father made him the luckiest man alive. If only everything in life was so clear.

"Glad you're here, sweetheart," he said into the baby's smile. "Want to go on a treasure hunt with me and Laura?"

A beaming Katy broke in. "Annie just had a bottle and needs a nap. Why don't I take care of her for you?"

Sam caught Annie's tiny fingers before she poked him in the eye. "What do you think, sport? Want to take a nap?"

Annie gurgled and tried again, this time for his other eye. "Guess you'd better take her," Sam said reluctantly. "I'm going to need two eyes for this job."

"Sure." With a soft murmur, Katy took back the baby. "If that treasure turns out to be diamonds, don't forget to count me in."

"You wish." Sam kissed Annie's cheek and reluctantly turned back to Laura. "Where do we start looking?"

Hank scratched his beard. "Recollect there's a passel of boxes of Jonah's stuff stashed in a corner of the barn."

"The barn? Hell of a place to keep valuables. Know what's in those boxes, Laura?"

She shook her head. "Mom used to say Dad never threw away anything with writing on it. I know *I* never paid much attention to what he was doing."

Sam hid a smile. Jonah Evans sounded as if he'd marched to the beat of a different drummer.

"How about you, Hank? Do *you* know what's in those boxes?"

Hank shrugged. "Nope. Mind my own business."

"Then I guess we'll have to start with the barn." With Laura and Pete Dolan at his heels, Sam started down the porch stairs.

They were intercepted by a Calhoun General Merchandise delivery truck. Sam bit back a curse. The last thing they needed was Montgomery's chief gossip showing up in the middle of a search for tax receipts. The guy's timing couldn't have been worse.

"Mornin'." Calhoun emerged from his truck with an innocuous smile on his face, but Sam wasn't fooled. The guy's eyes were taking in every detail.

"Morning," Sam echoed. "Making a delivery?"

"Yeah." Calhoun craned his neck and looked over Sam's shoulder at the sheriff. "Trouble?"

To Sam's relief, Pete Dolan ambled up. "No trouble. Just visiting. How about you?"

Sam could tell Calhoun wasn't convinced. No wonder. There were more people standing around the yard talking than there were sheep munching their lunch out in the meadow. Considering what was going on, he couldn't blame the man. Not after he'd probably passed Magraw's car on the way in and added everything up.

"Making a delivery." Calhoun turned an interested gaze on Laura. "If you're really starting a camp, guess sheep ranching didn't pay off, after all.''

"Not enough," Laura agreed. "That's where the supplies come in."

Calhoun glanced around him. "Got the place looking better than it has in years. When's this camp supposed to start up?"

"It's *going* to start as soon as school's out for Easter break," Laura answered firmly. "And in case you're wondering why I didn't spread the word, I wanted to pretty much keep the camp to myself. That is, until I was sure I had some takers."

"That ought to give us some time to..." Sam began. When he saw Calhoun focus on him, he bit back the rest of his sentence.

Sure enough, Calhoun picked up on Sam's hesitation. "Time to do what?"

"Time to put things in order for the campers. I know you're busy back at the store," Sam added with a pointed look at the delivery truck. "Need any help unloading?"

"Nah. Ain't that much." Calhoun fumbled in his pocket and pulled out an envelope. "Say, Laura," he began hesitantly, "I know you've always had a running account with me, but seeing as how I heard..."

"Heard what?" From the tone of Calhoun's voice, Laura had an inkling what was coming. The word, courtesy of Magraw, had to be out that the Lazy E ranch was on the verge of foreclosure.

"Spit it out, Nate," Pete Dolan broke in. "Just what did you hear?"

"That the county's getting ready to call in overdue taxes, and Laura's about to lose the ranch. It's only hearsay," Calhoun hurried to add at Laura's outraged gasp. "I was sorry to hear it, Laura, but business is business. I got to ask for cash on delivery for these supplies."

Sam shot Calhoun a withering look, pulled her aside and shielded her with his body from Calhoun's view. When she looked up at him, he pulled a hundred-dollar bill from his wallet. "Here. I'm sure I owe you more rent for taking me and Annie in. If it isn't enough, there's more where that came from."

Laura muttered a protest. "No thanks. I couldn't take advantage of you like this. We both know the accident wasn't all your fault. The road's a mess."

Sam could feel Calhoun's avid gaze boring into his back. No way was he going to let the jackass get away with putting Laura on the spot or taking back the camp supplies. "Sure it was. I should have been paying closer attention to the condition of the road."

"I almost did the same thing myself yesterday, remember?" Laura pushed his hand away. "Besides, you said Annie cried."

Sam took her hand, folded the money inside and closed her fingers over it. "Humor me."

Laura couldn't resist the appeal in his voice or the real concern for her in his eyes. To her growing dismay, it was a concern that clearly went beyond the boundaries of mere friendship.

The Sam Harrison she was beginning to know was a revelation, and she wasn't sure what to do about it. All the reasons she'd given herself for keeping her emotional distance from the man still applied. Only, the reasons didn't seem that important anymore. Probably because of the stepped-up beating of her heart as he gazed tenderly down at her. She smiled her thanks and marched back to Calhoun. "How much?"

Calhoun had the grace to look apologetic, but to Sam's disgust, the man didn't back off. "Ninety-eight dollars and sixteen cents."

Laura handed over the money and fixed the storekeeper with a frosty look. "You can apply the change toward the ranch account."

Calhoun grinned weakly, nodded his thanks and went to work unloading the truck.

With Calhoun safely out of the way, Pete Dolan cleared his throat and spoke up. "Well, Sam, if there wasn't any truth behind the gossip about something going on between you and Laura before this, there sure is now."

"Damn!" Sam smacked his forehead. "I should have thought about how things would look. The truth is, all I could think of was getting rid of Calhoun."

"Yeah, damn," Dolan echoed dryly. "I'd better get this stuff up to the house. You and Laura get started looking for those receipts."

"Let me help you, Pete. I'm going there, anyway." Katy reached for a shopping bag and winked at the sheriff. "How about you, Hank? Want to help?"

"Sorry. Gotta help with those boxes." Hank scurried toward the barn as fast as his boots would take him.

"Looks as if Katy's taken with you, Pete," Laura said under her breath. "You should feel flattered. I haven't known Katy to take to a man this quickly before." She glanced over at Sam and smiled. "Sam, too. But that's probably because you're Annie's father."

Sam bowed his thanks. "Can't think of a better reason."

"Depends on which side of the fence you're sitting on." Pete winced and hefted two bulging shopping bags filled with wrapped packages. "I've been a bachelor for more than fifty years, and I aim to keep it that way. 'Course," he added as he headed for the house, ''got to admit Katy's a fine-looking woman.''

Laura watched Pete trudge up the steps. ''Seems to me that no matter what Pete says, he's happy around Katy. He's probably not met a strong woman like her before, or he wouldn't be so sure he's going to be able to resist her.''

Sam studied Pete's disappearing figure and mentally paired him off with Katy. ''Ought to be interesting at that.''

''Pete doesn't know it yet, but his bachelor days are over,'' Laura laughingly agreed. ''A woman like Katy knows when the right man comes along.''

''Sounds as if you might be two of a kind,'' Sam replied as they headed for the barn. ''You're both pretty strong when the chips are down.''

''We are a lot alike,'' Laura agreed absently, ''especially when it comes to children. But not when it comes to men.''

''Why not?''

''Because I'm not looking,'' Laura answered as they entered the barn.

Why Laura wasn't looking when she was such an attractive woman puzzled Sam. And like every other puzzle he'd encountered in his life, he intended to solve it.

The barn smelled old and musty. When Sam's eyes adjusted to the dim light, he noticed an old dray wagon with the driver's seat gone occupying a corner. Kerosene lamps hung from the wooden pillars. A stack of horse blankets and worn leather harnesses spoke of a time when the Lazy E had been a thriving ranch. Vintage farm tools, still in decent shape, were scattered everywhere. Several pairs of worn cowboy boots were neatly lined up against a wall.

A faint pungent horse smell lingered, although the only horse Sam had noticed on the ranch was the one Laura had been riding the other day.

Laura's mother had been right, Sam thought with a rueful smile as he surveyed articles that represented Jonah Evans's lifetime of hard work as a sheep rancher. Evans might not have been able to throw anything away, but useful or not, each item had its own story to tell.

Drawing on his keen sense of history, Sam pictured the dray being pulled by a team of horses on hay rides and picnics. The kerosene lamps would have been used to light the living room where his wife read aloud during the long winter nights. The worn harnesses spoke of the days when horses had been the prime method of transportation for a man who didn't trust progress, including banks.

As far as Sam could see, there were no baby items, toys or a crib. But he did notice a children's bicycle that had been lovingly tucked into a corner and protected from the elements by a small patchwork quilt. Probably Laura's just after she'd been adopted.

It looked as if every item Jonah Evans kept had had some special meaning for him.

Sam sighed and turned away. The irony of it all was that many of the things Sam was looking at were collector's items. His hands itched to hold a camera and photograph the interior of the old barn for posterity.

Did Laura realize the treasure trove hidden here? A treasure trove that certainly could pay the current land taxes many times over? Assuming she would be willing to part with them. The bigger problem was paying past due taxes, if they turned out to be still due.

"The boxes are over here under a tarp, Sam," Laura called from the other side of the barn. "Pete's uncovering them now."

"Coming." Sam reluctantly tore himself away from the antique spice cabinet he'd found hidden away under the stack of blankets. He'd seen one just like it in the Smithsonian in D.C. a few years ago. He lingered long enough to open a couple of drawers and found them filled with nuts, bolts and screws. He rolled his eyes at the sacrilege and headed for the opposite corner of the barn.

Laura and Hank had their heads together examining a stack of cardboard boxes where time and the weather had done its work. As far as Sam could tell, most of the boxes looked as if one good shove would make them explode and scatter their contents over the floor of the barn. "Any of the boxes dated? We could check out the latest one first."

"No. I'm afraid the only way to decide which is the most recent box is by the condition of the box. Unfortunately none of them look too sturdy. Well," Laura added with a grimace, "guess we'd better get started."

Two grimy hours later, it was clear to Sam that the boxes didn't contain tax receipts or anything of value except to Jonah Evans himself. And that trouble came in pairs.

Chapter Six

Sam eyed the contents of the boxes. Stiff with age, dusty and even water-logged, they were useless. "If I were seventy-five and I didn't trust banks," he finally said thoughtfully, "I don't think I'd keep important papers in the barn. Odds and ends that might have some meaning to me, maybe, but not official documents."

Laura paused in her examination of a rain-stained manila envelope. "You're right. I know my father. The more precious the document, I think, the closer Dad would have kept it. But where?"

"If it were me, I'd pick a place closer to home where I could keep an eye on valuable papers. Someplace where they'd be safe and protected from the elements, not in a barn." Sam tossed a decade-old newspaper onto the pile of papers they'd already examined. "Is there a place like that in the house?"

"The basement of course!" Laughing, Laura got

to her feet. "Dad had an old steamer trunk he picked up at a flea market. It smelled so bad Mom wouldn't let him keep it in the house, so he kept it down there. I should have thought of it before now."

"Then that's where we'll search next." Sam glanced at the stacks of papers and newspapers they'd already looked through. "Some historical society might want to take a look at this stuff. Why don't you put the tarp over it, Hank? We'll look at it again later. There might be something here Laura would like to keep for herself."

"Sure," Hank answered sourly. "Gotta keep it out of sight, anyway. After those campers show up, there's no telling what they might get into."

Laura laughed again. "Go on, Hank. You know you're looking forward to working with the children. You said so yourself when I told you my idea about a camp."

"Yeah," Hank answered. "Guess kids aren't too different from sheep, anyway. Tame one and the rest will follow."

Laura rolled her eyes at Hank's pragmatic philosophy. As far as she knew, outside of herself, Hank had never had any contact with children. "Come on, Sam. Let's leave this for Hank and go find that trunk."

True to Laura's memory, the steamer trunk smelled of camphor and mildew and was stiff as a board.

Drawer after drawer was filled with pictures and journals her father had kept through his years of ranching. But to her regret, there were no records of tax payments or receipts.

"Maybe you don't have to worry about finding receipts, after all," Sam said when they finally stopped for a break. "As far as I can see, there are enough antiques and historical newspapers in the barn to run your own antiques road show. Ought to be more than enough to pay back taxes."

"Probably," Laura said, gently rubbing a snapshot of herself as a teenage girl atop her favorite horse. "I just hate to get rid of something that meant so much to Dad and to me."

Laura smiled sadly as she leafed through a journal dated ten years earlier. "They're full of memories. Dad left all this to me for a reason. It's hard to explain," she went on as she wiped away the tears that formed in the corners of her eyes. "I used to live in a series of foster homes where nothing really belonged to me. Having all this and what's in the barn makes me feel as if I've belonged here forever. Dad must have known they'd mean a lot to me."

"Then don't sell. At least, not until you have to," Sam said sympathetically. There were times in his life when he'd been adrift, and only warm memories of his own father kept him going. "If you don't mind talking about it, what happened to your birth parents?''

"I don't mind," she answered. "It was a long time ago. They were killed in an automobile accident when I was ten. I was spending the weekend with a friend, and there was a snowstorm. My parents were on their way to bring me home when they were caught by an avalanche.'' When she looked up at Sam, her eyes swam with tears. "I've never forgiven myself for insisting on going to my friend's house for a sleepover.''

Sam clasped her hand in his and remembered the last time he'd seen his own father. And the terrible sense of loss he'd felt afterward. "You couldn't have known there would be an avalanche. You were only a kid, right?''

"Yes, ten." Laura said. "I spent the next two years in foster homes until I was finally adopted.'' She showed Sam a snapshot. "The first thing my new father did was give me a horse. He decided I was a tomboy at heart and set out to let me be one. He was right. At twelve, I thought the horse was more exciting than dolls.''

"It sounds as if your father was a great guy."

"He was. Mom, too,'' Laura said sadly. "Unfortunately she only lasted a year after we lost Dad to a heart attack.'' She put the snapshot in her jeans pocket. "That's the reason I hate to sell anything that reminds me of them."

"Then don't," Sam said again, then pulled out the last drawer of the steamer trunk. "We'll just have to keep looking or find another way to pay the taxes."

They were interrupted by the ring of the telephone upstairs. Laura jumped to her feet. "Be back in a minute."

When she didn't return as promised, Sam went upstairs to look for her. She was curled up on the couch, her face white, the telephone in her listless hand. "Who called? Is anything wrong?"

"It was Pete. He wanted me to know there's a rumor around town that I was never legally adopted." The stricken look in her eyes made Sam want to shoot someone.

He cursed under his breath. Laura's troubles were suddenly adding up. No way could it be sheer coincidence. He took the telephone out of Laura's hands and dropped on to the couch beside her. "Where did that rumor come from?"

"Pete told me he was taking a coffee break down at Josie's Diner. Said he heard Edna Morris, a clerk at the county courthouse, talking about a couple of men nosing around old adoption records. By the time Pete came in, word had spread that I was the subject of the search."

"Jeez! No wonder you look so pale. Too bad Pete didn't wait until he had a chance to check the rumor out."

"Pete's a dear friend," Laura said tonelessly. "He wanted to give me a chance to find my adoption papers before anything actually happened. As for who was looking through the records at the courthouse, Pete's pretty sure it was some of Hansen's men. Magraw can't be the only one on the man's payroll."

Sam thought about it for a long moment. Missing tax receipts were bad enough, but taking Laura in without a legal adoption? "Is there a chance your father didn't go through a legal adoption?"

Laura looked at him through unshed tears.

Sam was deeply moved by Laura's sadness. Aware she felt she was losing her beloved father one more time, he put his arm around her. He pulled her close and buried his lips in her hair.

No one should have to lose their parents twice, he thought, let alone their legal identity. And for an orphaned child, it was bound to be traumatic.

He thought of his own heartache and how helpless he'd felt after he'd lost his father. He, at least, had a mother to love and guide him.

When Laura looked up at him questioningly, Sam gave in to his need to show her she wasn't alone. He bent and kissed the corner of one of her eyes.

"Don't worry, we don't know the truth. Not yet, anyway. I'm sure Pete will let us know the minute he gets the facts. We'll take it from there."

Laura gazed up at him. "Don't feel sorry for me," she said through her tears. "I don't think I can bear it."

"I don't feel sorry for you, Laura," Sam murmured softly as he gently brushed her cheeks with his fingers. "I care for you." He pressed her closer to him and did what he'd wanted to do ever since he'd first laid eyes on her. He kissed her.

His first attraction to Laura had been instinctive, a man-and-woman thing. Now, two days later, things had changed. His affection for her grew as he began to see the real woman.

Laura was strong because she had to be, loving because she wanted to be. And caring because it was the only way a genuine woman like her could be.

He'd never wanted a woman the way he wanted this one.

He kissed away Laura's tears, then her lips again. Gently at first, then with all the emotion that had pent up inside him the past couple of days. "I care," he repeated softly. "We'll get through together."

Laura looked into Sam's compassionate eyes and recognized the truth. Sam not only cared, he recognized that she needed someone to hold her. That he was that someone.

She knew next to nothing about the man, only that a spring rain and some divine intervention appeared to have sent him to her. And that she wanted him in all the ways a woman wants a man. With a contented sigh, she nestled closer to him. Smiling through her tears, she closed her eyes and lost herself in Sam's kiss.

The taste of him, his maleness, his musky scent and his strong arms around her filled a void in her heart she'd ignored too long. Foolishly ignored because she'd believed she wasn't a complete woman.

In Sam's embrace, all her feminine instincts were aroused. His touch on the bare skin of her throat was too sensual to ignore. The tenderness in the way he looked at her told her he thought she was a woman in all the ways a woman can be. The woman she'd been afraid to be. Coherent thought fled as she drowned herself in the magic of his kiss.

"Katy," she murmured when she realized the kiss was turning into something more.

"Katy didn't answer the telephone, so she must be outside with Annie," Sam answered with a shaky laugh. He brushed her cheek with the back of his knuckles to wipe the last of her tears away. "There's no one here but the two of us. Besides, this *is* just a kiss, isn't it?"

Laura knew better. Deep in her heart, she realized Sam's kiss could easily become more than just a kiss; she wanted more. Until she realized that even if Sam eventually turned out to be the right man for her, it was the wrong time and the wrong place.

How could she put aside the truth and still be honest with herself? And more importantly, how could she be honest with Sam?

Shaken by her response to Sam, she made herself pull out of his arms. "I'm sorry. I'm afraid I got carried away. I can't let Hansen get away with this nonsense." She looked up at Sam and smiled. "I'll be okay as soon as I get my act together."

Bewildered at the abrupt change in Laura, Sam let her go. There had to be time later to show her how much he had begun to care for her. No way did he want her to think he was taking advantage of her heartache. "Are you sure you want this to end this way?"

She bit her lower lip. Sure? After the way she'd felt in Sam's arms? How could she be sure of anything? If he was bewildered by her hot and cold actions, so was she. She ought to have known better than to lose control. A nurse, she may have learned to keep her emotions under control, but she was on the verge of losing that control now.

"I have to be," she answered, willing her body to cool, her mind to return to important matters. "We'd better get back to looking for those tax receipts, or I *will* be in deep trouble." And not only for tax receipts, she thought wildly. "As for my adoption certificate, I'm not sure I know where to look for it. No one has ever asked to see it before."

Sam nodded reluctantly. Although he ached to take Laura back into his arms and make love to her until smiles replaced her tears, she was probably right. He'd promised himself to help her find tax receipts, not to take advantage of her vulnerability.

As for himself, maybe it was too soon after his divorce even to think of becoming involved with another woman. Even a magical woman like Laura. But Annie had to come first—although that wouldn't stop him from helping Laura now that she needed him.

He pulled Laura to her feet and forced a smile to hide his regret that their embrace was over. "Got it. I'll be down in the basement. Come on down when you're ready."

Laura watched Sam disappear through the door leading to the basement. She wouldn't have blamed him if he'd thought she was out of her mind.

She glanced around at the silent house. A silence that seemed to close in around her. With Sam at work in the basement, she needed to get outdoors to think clearly, to share her thoughts with someone who understood her. Not only about the need for her adoption certificate, but about Sam and where his unexpected attraction was taking her. After a longing look at the door to the basement, she headed outside for Katy's pragmatic advice.

She found her friend in the lawn swing with Annie in her arms.

"Found anything yet?"

"No." Laura dropped onto the swing, and Annie's bright smile welcomed her. "Annie's always happy, isn't she?" she said wistfully. "I hope she stays that way."

"She will, unless she's wet or hungry." Katy plopped Annie in Laura's lap. "Here you go. The kid's the best medicine for the blues I can think of." She waited a few moments while Laura played peek-a-boo with the baby. "Something on your mind? Besides tax receipts, that is."

With a push of her toe, Laura nodded and sent the lawn swing in motion. "Annie's father."

"What about Annie's father?"

Laura buried her face in Annie's soft-as-down hair. "I think I like him."

Katy laughed. "Me, too." She glanced sharply at Laura's troubled eyes. "Guess you like Sam in a different way than I do. So what's the problem? Afraid Sam doesn't return the feeling?"

"No. I'm afraid he does." Laura sighed ruefully. "It's just that I don't think it's fair to Sam to let myself become too involved with him. He has his work to do, and I have the ranch to take care of. I don't even know how long he intends to stick around here. Either way, it's a no-win situation.''

Katy nodded wisely. "For him or for you?"

"Both," Laura replied. "But especially for Sam."

Katy smiled, a knowing smile. "I know you too well to buy that story, Laura. You have more to offer a man than most women do." She gestured to Annie, busily playing with the colored buttons on Laura's shirt. "Something tells me you're talking about not being able to have children of your own. It's a little too soon to think about that, isn't it?"

Too soon? Laura thought. *Maybe.* "I know." She fondled the cleft in Annie's chin with her thumb. "But I would love to have a child like this one someday." *Sam's child, if fate hasn't decreed otherwise.*

Katy wiped the drool off Annie's lips with a fresh tissue. "Seems to me it's too soon to worry about more babies. If and when the time comes, why don't you let Sam decide for himself? For now, why don't you think of him as a friend?"

"Decide what for myself?" Sam said as he joined them. Laura blushed. Katy cleared her throat. Annie's face broke into a wide smile and she reached her arms out for her father.

Laura watched Sam and his infant daughter together. She was struck again by the way Annie, with her tiny upturned nose, resembled her father. The same clear chocolate-brown eyes, golden-brown hair, the same crooked grin that melted a woman's heart and the same cleft in her chin.

"Whether to stick around here or leave when your replacement car gets here," Laura said brightly. "I'm sure you're anxious to get on with the photo shoot at the spa."

To Annie's delight, Sam swung her high into the air. "I'm not that anxious to get back to work," he answered as he laughed up into Annie's sparkling eyes. "I'm staying, at least until things settle down around here." He looked questioningly at Laura. "That is, if you still want me around...."

The way Laura and Katy exchanged guilty glances made him wonder just what the two had really been talking about when he'd strolled up. After all, hadn't he already told Laura he was staying as long as it took to help her?

Katy jumped to her feet. "Here, let me take that baby before she upchucks her lunch. She needs a diaper change and a nap." With a meaningful glance at Laura, Katy marched up to the house.

Empty-handed, Sam stood gazing after Katy. "What was that all about?"

Aware Katy was diplomatically attempting to give her a moment alone with Sam, Laura shrugged.

There were more important things to worry about right now than falling in love. "Find anything?"

"Not yet." Sam dropped onto the swing. "I've been thinking. Maybe you ought to go to the bank in Montgomery and find out if your father decided to trust the banks, after all."

"Hardly. Not after the banks closed during the depression."

"I guess there's always the proverbial mattress," Sam said with a grin. "Heard some people hid their valuables there after the banks failed."

"Now I know you're kidding. No one has been in mom and dad's bedroom since mom passed away two years ago. Besides," she confessed with a rueful smile, "I already looked."

"Oh, I don't know." Sam got to his feet and pulled her toward the house. "Got any spare bedrooms? Maybe a bed or two that haven't been used?"

"A few—six." Laura answered, almost running to keep up with him. "Dad told me the ranch house was built over a hundred years ago when large families were needed to work on the land. That's how I came up with the plan for the camp."

She led the way into the house and up to a bedroom at the back of the second floor. Inside were twin whitewashed wooden beds, each neatly covered with a patchwork quilt. A wooden stand in a corner held a white porcelain pitcher and a basin. Shutters covered the closed windows. A musty smell filled the air.

When Sam sneezed, Laura rushed to open the shutters, and fresh air flowed inside. "We can start with this bedroom and work our way back down the hall, excluding my room and yours. I cleared out your bedroom to put in the bunk beds, so I know there's nothing hidden there."

Sam gazed around the room. A sense of its emptiness filled him. "I don't think we'll find anything here," he said slowly, and started to turn away.

"How do you know?" Laura held back and frowned as she glanced around the room. "We haven't had a chance to look under the mattresses."

"Call it a sixth sense," Sam answered. "Or maybe," he said with an unashamed grin, "because there's dust an inch thick on the quilts. The beds look as if they haven't been disturbed in years."

Laura gazed at the twin beds. "Maybe, but I don't think we ought to rule it out without checking to make sure."

"Okay," Sam said cheerfully. "You take one side of the mattress nearest you, and I'll take the other. It ought to be easy enough to see if there's anything between the mattress and the box spring."

Dust flew when they lifted the first mattress. It

was Laura's turn to sneeze. "You're right. You'd make a good detective."

"Not really," Sam answered. "It's just that I have a photographer's eye for detail. In my line of work, it's the details that other people don't see that count." He gazed at her suggestively.

Laura felt as though he saw more of her than met his eyes. She blushed. "There are three more bedrooms to check. Let's go."

"Got it," Sam answered with a crooked grin. "Lead on."

The next bedroom turned out to have an even dustier smell. "Guess I'm not a very good housekeeper," Laura managed through a series of sneezes. "With all I've had to do to get the house ready for the campers, I'm afraid I haven't taken the time."

"Not to worry. Maybe the next one will be it," Sam said as he eyed the bed, shrugged and headed for the door.

Laura followed him into the next bedroom. "That sixth sense of yours again?"

"No, just the evidence," he remarked over his shoulder. "Lots of dust, no footsteps." He walked into the bedroom, took a close look at the double bed and pointed to one corner of the quilt that covered it. "This quilt's been disturbed. Not recently, because I can see there's a thin layer of dust here.

Just not as thick as there was on the last three. Here, grab the other side of the mattress, and let's take a good look.''

And there between the mattress and the box spring, in a neat pile, they found two bundles of official-looking papers neatly bound with thin straps of leather.

''Thank goodness!'' Laura said. She helped Sam move the mattress off the bed and grabbed the packages. ''I was sure there wasn't anything terribly wrong with Dad.'' She handed Sam one package and untied the other. ''Thank goodness—tax receipts. What are yours?''

''Income-tax returns, filled out in longhand,'' Sam replied. ''Guess your father didn't put much faith in accountants, either. No wonder you haven't had a visit from the IRS or the county tax collector.''

''I think you're right,'' Laura answered with a relieved smile. ''Dad used to say he went to the school of hard knocks. He also used to say the sure way to do something right was to learn how to do it and then do it yourself,'' she added happily. ''I learned a lot the hard way, including how to ride a horse and shear a sheep. Anyway, I was sure all along Dad paid his taxes.'' Laura clutched the official-looking papers to her chest.

Sam smiled. Thank God, this time Laura's tears

were happy ones. "So that means someone lied or altered the tax records," Sam said thoughtfully. "Or maybe arranged to have them altered."

"Hansen?"

"Probably," Sam answered. "Unless you've had other offers to purchase." She shook her head. "I'll have a talk with Pete, tell him what we found and ask him to look into it. In the meantime you'd better take these, make sure they're recorded and put them in a safe-deposit box. You do have one, don't you?"

"I will now," Laura answered with a grin. "As soon as the bank opens on Monday."

"What happens next?"

Laura's gaze locked with Sam's. The look in his warm brown eyes had turned wary. Wary because they both knew that now that the missing tax receipts had been found, he could be on his way.

Or, if she listened to what her thundering heart was telling her, she could give him an answer that would invite him to stay.

Chapter Seven

Laura knew she should be concentrating on important matters, not on Sam and what his gaze was doing to her. She gazed at Sam silently. At the rate she was falling in love with him, she didn't have a chance of accomplishing anything else. Instead, she yearned for the strength of his arms around her, the warmth of his smile and the sharing of his can-do approach to life.

The problem seemed to be that her heart wasn't listening to her head. "There's always the camp," she said to him casually. "It would help if you were here to get things set up before the campers arrive. That is, if you really don't have to leave right away."

Sam's lips curved in the lopsided smile that melted her bones. "Annie and I will be happy to stick around."

"You would?" she asked, pleased at his answer

and wondering at the same time if she was doing the right thing.

"Sure," he said with a sheepish grin. "I need a few more lessons on taking care of Annie, anyway. Annie's not going to be six months old forever. She's bound to need more than clean diapers and three bottles a day."

"You're worrying for nothing," Laura answered with a sympathetic smile. "Babies aren't really that much of a deal. They manage to survive in spite of us."

"You've a lot more experience than I do. How am I going to teach her to eat real food, let alone talk or walk?" he asked worriedly. "If I'd known I might wind up being a full-time father, I would have read a few books on parenting."

Sam looked so serious it was hard for Laura to keep from laughing at him. If only he knew how afraid she'd been with the first babies in her care.

As a maternity-ward nurse, she'd known hundreds of nervous new fathers, and Sam fit the stereotype to a T. "I assure you, Annie will do what comes naturally to babies. All *you* have to do is let her do for herself. Your big part in this is to make sure she's healthy. And from the way you drive," she added dryly, "to always make sure she's safely buckled into a car seat. Oh, and one more important thing."

Sam looked more apprehensive than ever. "What's that?"

"It's really very simple," she answered softly. "Let her know you love her."

"That's easy. I do, and I already have," Sam said with a sigh of relief.

The tender look that came over Sam's face when he spoke of loving Annie warmed Laura's heart. She mentally added to a growing list another reason for his attraction.

"As for my helping with the campers, I was a Boy Scout when I was a kid. Even became a Star Scout," Sam added proudly. "I'm a pro at this camping business. Keeping six little kids in line ought to be easy."

"You wish." Laura laughed at Sam's naiveté. "You're just like Hank. I can hardly wait to see how you handle half-a-dozen restless young children. In spite of what Hank said, children aren't at all like sheep. You're going to find each one has a mind of his own."

"No problem," Sam assured her airily. "I'm looking forward to a change of pace. Annie is, too."

Laura lost the battle to keep her emotional distance from Sam. In the short time he'd been in her life, she'd not only come to grips with the woman in her, she was falling for the man who had woken her. Now, all she had to do was decide whether it was a case of actually falling in love or simply gratitude for his being there for her.

"Good," she said. "Now that that's settled, we can put the bed back together. I'll go down, call Pete and tell him what we've found." She lifted her end of the mattress to shove it back in place and motioned for Sam to lift the other end.

"No way," Sam chided playfully. He drew Laura to his side and put his arm around her. "Leave the bed to me. You can talk to Pete later. Right now I figure it's time to celebrate."

"Celebrate?" Laura began to wonder just what Sam meant and how far he intended the celebration to go. "What...what did you have in mind?"

He brushed her cheek with a gentle fingertip. "Not what you think, Annie Oakley, although it's certainly worth consideration."

Laura tried to be nonchalant, but her body warmed just being in Sam's arms. "Are you trying to tell me I'll be safe with you?"

"For now, anyway." His wicked grin belied his words.

"But you'll warn me if things change, won't you?" she asked, even as she sensed their relationship was changing faster than she could keep up with it. And that it was okay with her.

Sam sat down on the bed and put his arms behind him. "Look, I'll show you," he said. "I'm safe. In fact, you can do anything to me, and I won't touch you."

Laura's gaze locked with his. Her heart began to pound. Desire rushed to points south, and her body tingled with her response to Sam. "Anything?"

"Anything. Go ahead, try."

Gathering her courage, Laura brushed his cheek with her fingers the way he'd brushed hers. He didn't blink. She bent to his upturned face and kissed the mouth that curved in a lopsided smile. When she felt his lips respond to hers, she drew back. "Maybe that's enough for now."

"Yes," he agreed in a throaty voice that told her he was just as affected by the near kiss as she was. She gazed at him quizzically, wondering where to go from here.

Seeing the color rise on those beautiful cheeks, Sam took pity on Laura. "How about settling for a pot of hot black-as-sin coffee to toast our finding the tax receipts?"

Part of Laura was relieved at his unexpected suggestion; part of her was deeply disappointed. Every inch of her wanted Sam, just as much as the look in his eyes and his questing lips had told her he wanted her. But there was a problem—two problems, actually.

She couldn't afford to let herself fall for Sam, to hope for a possible future together. Not when he had one child and might want another. A child she couldn't give him.

Twenty-first-century thinking or not, there was still the second problem. She wasn't the type to go for a one-night stand.

"Of course," she answered as she backed away. "I wasn't thinking of anything more."

Coffee was safe, Laura mused as she closed her mind to the unspoken challenge in Sam's eyes. The truth was, she felt more like celebrating with a glass of champagne and another of Sam's heart-stopping kisses than black coffee. And considering the way desire was spreading through her, maybe more. She sighed and pulled out of Sam's arms. "Too bad there's not a bottle of champagne handy. I'm afraid coffee will have to do."

Sam lounged against the doorjamb and admired Laura as she skipped down the stairs. On the surface she resembled a strong woman without a care in the world, but he knew better. Inside that beautiful façade there lurked a vulnerable woman.

He'd known his share of strong women, but Laura Evans was at the top of the list. He didn't know what her ranch was actually worth in dollars, but he was pretty sure a lesser woman would have sold out by now and enjoyed the good life. But then, he reminded himself, Laura obviously wasn't a lesser kind of woman.

He pushed the mattress into place, straightened the quilt and surveyed the bedroom. Somewhere during their search, Laura had mentioned that the bedroom on the other side of the door was hers. With little campers coming, he was happy to give up his bunk bed. And maybe take this room, the room next to Laura's. The change might try a man's soul. He had to remember why he was here: to help Laura.

The prospect of a house full of children was daunting. He'd have to make believe the ranch was a Boy Scout camp to make it work. And he'd have to make it clear he was the man in charge.

The picture of Annie as a miniature Girl Scout and himself as a Scout leader sitting around a log fire singing one of the Scouts' favorite camp songs, "My Darling Clementine," tickled the hell out of him. The mental picture of a grown Annie tickled him more.

With a last thoughtful look at the bed and the secret knowledge it wasn't the prospect of sitting around a Scout campfire with Laura that was pleasing him, he whistled his way to the kitchen.

"I've been thinking." He sat down at the kitchen table and inhaled the cup of freshly perked coffee waiting for him. "We have to talk."

Laura paused in the process of pouring herself a cup of coffee. "About what?"

"About Hansen. Saw a land-auction notice when we were in Montgomery and wondered why he's so determined to have your ranch."

Laura set a plate of shortbread cookies in front of him, reached into the refrigerator for a small jug of cream for herself and joined him at the table. "Because most of the land around here comes with strings attached."

Sam bit into a cookie and sighed contentedly. "Great! Homemade?"

"Glad you like it, and yes, it is." A dimple danced across her cheek as she poured cream into her coffee. "Baking is one of my hobbies. That and spinning my own wool."

Sam polished off the crisp cookie and reached for another. "The campers are going to love you," he said with relish. He licked crumbs off his lips and took another swallow of coffee. "What did you mean by strings?"

Laura blinked. The sight of Sam's tongue brushing cookie crumbs off his lips sent shafts of electricity through her. She sipped her coffee and forced herself to concentrate on his question.

She tried, but kept picturing the frank desire in his eyes when he'd offered his playful challenge. Brushing his lips with her own hadn't been like her, but then, she hadn't felt like her old self since Sam had taken out her fence.

She tried to concentrate on his question. "The Montgomery County Planning Commission recently announced they intend to rezone land use, and soon. Said they wanted to preserve the old ranch way of life."

Sam whistled and held out his empty cup for a refill. "No wonder Hansen is in such a hurry! Will the rezoning affect your ranch or the New Horizons Spa?"

Laura reached for the coffeepot and poured coffee. "Not the Lazy E so far, but it might make a difference once the zoning change goes into effect. As for the spa, they applied for and received a zoning variance after they discovered a hot springs on the property several years ago."

Silence fell in the kitchen as Sam thoughtfully sipped his coffee and made another foray into the plate of cookies. Outside, the dog barked excitedly. Sam relaxed. Katy and Annie must be outside with the animal. As long as they were together, Annie was in good hands.

"By the way," he asked, "does the mutt have a name?"

Laura frowned. "She's not a mutt, and her name is Fancy."

"Fancy it is," Sam said. "Too bad she's not more particular about who shows up here. No, not me," he laughingly protested. "I was thinking of Hansen and Magraw. Too bad she didn't take a bite of them. But back to the reason for my question. Does Hansen still have time to turn the Lazy E into a dump site?''

''Over my dead body,'' Laura retorted, her gaze cold. ''The Lazy E has been a sheep ranch for more than one hundred years, and as far as I'm concerned, it's going to remain that way.'' Her eyes narrowed. Her mouth turned grim. Sam almost felt sorry for Hansen. The poor guy didn't know what was in store for him the next time he showed up.

''Maybe this used to be a sheep ranch, but it doesn't look like one now,'' Sam said. ''I remember seeing a small flock of sheep grazing somewhere. What happened to the rest of the herd?''

''Mom and I sold off most of it when Dad died. I was still working, and Mom didn't have the heart to keep going. We kept a small herd for their wool,'' she said softly. Sam saw the sadness that crossed Laura's face. His mother had reacted the same way after his own father had been killed.

His heart ached for Laura as he covered her hand with his and toyed with her fingers. ''Unless you have another herd hidden somewhere, you don't have enough sheep left to make the ranch pay its own way, let alone take care of your next tax bill.'' He paused, afraid he was about to offend Laura, but determined to make his offer. "I have some money saved up. Let me help you."

"No thanks," she answered proudly. She drew her hand away and grasped her cup. "I told you I was raised to do for myself, and I will. I still have enough sheep left to sell their wool to a clientele of hobbyists. They come here every year to pick up newly sheared wool or the wool I've spun. Between my leftover nursing salary, the sale of the wool and the camp, I'm sure I'll be able to pay expenses. And taxes, too."

Sam was fascinated by the mental picture of Laura spinning wool or working at a loom against a backdrop of a blazing fireplace and a winter storm outside. A page out of the past, unusual and touching in today's world.

His thoughts turned to a photo-journal article: life on a modern-day sheep ranch. With the verdant pastures of the picturesque ranch and the snowcapped mountains in the background, the article was bound to be a heck of a lot more interesting than pictures of a spa where rich people came to vegetate. "Who does the shearing?"

"The herd is small enough for Hank and a couple of old friends of his to take care of it. They were here last week."

The picture of three elderly men tackling the job of shearing reluctant squirming sheep made Sam even more fascinated. "Like in the movie *The Thorn Birds?* You know, the scene where there's this huge shearing shed and the characters hold the sheep between their legs and use electric shears to do the job?"

"Yes, like in *Thorn Birds,*" she laughingly agreed. "Only on a much-smaller scale. Hank's persuaded his friends Al and Jim to stick around and help out with the camp. They're gone now, but they'll be back next week."

Sam nodded thoughtfully and munched another cookie. With Katy, himself, Hank and his two friends to lend a hand, he was reasonably sure the camp was well on its way to becoming a paying proposition. If he added the proceeds of the photo journal he planned to put together depicting life on a sheep ranch, Laura wouldn't have to worry. Not this year, at least.

"That leaves us with the problem of Hansen and just how far he's willing to go to get your ranch," he said. "If you don't mind my asking, what was the guy's latest offer?"

"I don't mind. It was $3,100 an acre, but I'm still not interested."

Sam whistled. "Kind of high, isn't it?"

Laura sniffed. "That's because the Lazy E has abundant water running through it. I'm told dump sites need water to keep down dust and fumes."

"Interesting. How many acres do you have here?"

"Two hundred."

Sam mentally calculated the return. "That gives you $620,000. And maybe even a bonus to help persuade you to sell. Not bad, not bad at all."

"I don't care!" Laura's eyes flashed fire. "It could be a million dollars. This is my home. I'm still not interested."

"Maybe you could compromise," Sam added cautiously as he remembered the old rifle. Who knew what other weapons Laura had stashed around the ranch? Or if she was actually prepared to use them. "Maybe keep the house and a few acres for yourself?"

"On the edge of a dump site?" Laura's horrified reaction made Sam feel like a jackass. She was right. Who in their right mind would want to trade living on a property as beautiful as the Lazy E for a chance to live adjacent to a dump site spewing noxious fumes? And with noisy trucks passing by daily?

"Sorry," he said. "Since you won't let me help out financially, I just thought selling part of the ranch might solve some of your problems." He pushed back his chair, stood and stretched. "Guess I'll go see what Katy and Annie are doing. You can call Pete and see about getting the tax records cleared up."

Sam carried his cup to the sink and, with a cheery nod, wandered out of the kitchen.

Cup in hand, Laura watched Sam go. The unconscious sensuality in his stride fanned a stirring of desire she never remembered feeling before. She shook her head and cleared the table, unhappily aware Sam wasn't going to be easy to resist.

OUT IN THE YARD Sam drew a deep breath of the fresh air. The sun had dried out the mud, spring plants were pushing their way into the sunshine, and the weaving prairie grass surrounding the house looked greener than ever.

The ranch looked ready for an onslaught of six pairs of little feet. Maybe more, if the camp took off the way Laura hoped it would. Despite having been a Scout leader, the thought of a dozen young feet left him more than a little uneasy.

He found Katy coming out of the barn with Annie in her arms, the dog trotting at her heels. "Thought you both were going to take a nap."

"Yes, well, the little darling had different ideas, didn't you, pumpkin?" At the sight of her father, Annie grinned and reached out for Sam to take her. "I took her to see a bum lamb Hank is looking after in the barn."

Sam burst out laughing. "How could a lamb be

worthless? You gotta be putting me on!'' He paused when Katy shrugged. ''You are, aren't you?''

''Nope,'' Katy answered a grin. ''A bum lamb is a newborn lamb that's either been lost or rejected by its mother. Hank says they have one or two every year.''

With a sympathetic glance at the barn, Sam gathered his sleepy daughter in his arms. ''Looks like some human babies have the same problem, doesn't it?''

Katy eyed the baby fondly. ''Your ex-wife probably wasn't ready to be a mother. Thank goodness this little one has you. Lucky man, lucky little girl.''

''Hope Hank's better with little lambs than I am with babies,'' Sam said dryly. ''Laura's offered to give me a few pointers on the care and feeding of infants.''

Katy tilted her head and eyed him thoughtfully. ''Sounds to me as if you're seriously thinking about sticking around here. You are, aren't you?''

Sam breathed in Annie's clean baby scent and solemnly regarded Katy over the top of the baby's head. ''Thinking about it,'' he agreed. ''Depends on Laura.''

Annie cuddled more deeply into Sam's arms and with a murmur of contentment fell asleep against his shoulder. ''Looks as if Annie likes it here well enough to stay,'' he said softly, and kissed the top of her head.

Katy fell in beside him while they walked back to the house. ''Annie's a great calling card, Sam, but that's a long way from my being comfortable about your being good for Laura.'' She glanced up at Sam, her expression serious. ''Don't think I haven't noticed there's an attraction between the two of you. Fact is, I love Laura like a sister. I may have taken a shine to little Annie here, but frankly, Laura is my main concern. She's been through a lot. She deserves only the best. I wonder if you fit the bill.''

Sam realized he could give Katy the type of answer that included only a name, address—if he'd had a permanent one—and social-security number. For Laura's sake, he owed Katy more than that.

Katy was right. He and Laura did have sparks between them. There was also no denying the potential of those sparks to grow into a full-fledged bonfire.

''Fair enough,'' he replied. ''My name is really Sam Harrison—Samson, if you want to get formal. Privately,'' he added with a grimace, ''I hate the name, so I wish you wouldn't. I'm thirty-six, stayed clear of the law, am newly single and a photo-journalist by trade.''

''Don't stop there,'' Katy said, when he paused for breath. ''This is just starting to get interesting.''

Sam continued, "I've roamed all over the world. Not only for the adventure of it, but to photograph faraway places with strange-sounding names for posterity. Before what we laughingly call progress makes them disappear."

"And your marriage?"

Sam shrugged ruefully. "Pretty standard story, I guess. I fell in love with a beautiful airline attendant I'd crossed paths with a time or two and convinced myself it was time to settle down. Actually persuaded Paige to marry me. Somehow I wasn't able to convince the lady to settle for a home in Grand Junction, a couple of kids and Tuesday nights at the PTA."

He bent and kissed Annie again. "Maybe I just didn't have my head on straight. I blamed my ex for the mess we made of our marriage, but I was probably just as guilty as she was for not trying harder to make the marriage work. If it weren't for Annie, I'd say her mother was right. I just might turn out to be the kind of guy who needs to keep moving."

"Time will tell, won't it." Katy patted Sam on his arm. "Why don't you give the Lazy E a shot? Could be the ranch has everything a guy like you needs to make him want to park his walking boots." She turned away, stopped and turned back. "It's not me you have to convince, Sam. If you are serious about staying here, it might be a good idea to tell all this to Laura. She loves children. If you're the salesman I think you are and Laura the woman I know her to be, you might just manage to convince her that occasional nights at the PTA are worth considering. Just as long as she'll be able to spend the rest of the nights with you.'' She winked and walked on.

Sam wandered over to the lawn swing. With the sun shining on him, the swing was as good a place for thinking as any. As for Annie, she could sleep on his shoulder as easily as she did in the dresser drawer upstairs. He wasn't ready to go into the house. Not yet, anyway. He had a lot of thinking to do. And not all of it about his relationship with Laura.

He'd meant it when he'd told Katy that maybe he hadn't tried hard enough to make his marriage to Paige work. Once the honeymoon was over, he'd gone back to accepting assignments drawing him thousands of miles away from home. Paige hadn't understood his need to imprint strange and wonderful places. Any more than he'd understood her longing for adventure. She'd used his absence as the reason for their divorce, but in retrospect he realized Paige hadn't been any more prepared to set down roots than he had been.

He should have recognized the warning signals;

an airline attendant like his ex-wife had the same wanderlust in her blood as he had in his.

Although Annie hadn't been planned, he'd wanted children for most of his adult life. Not Paige; she hadn't been ready for motherhood.

He buried his lips in Annie's sweet-smelling hair. He loved his daughter, and sure, just as Laura had advised, he was willing to do anything to keep her safe and happy. But he had to face it: safe and happy meant putting down roots and seeing to it Annie was raised properly. It also meant a father and mother and maybe a sister or a brother. Maybe both.

That brought him back to Laura. The truth was that he was beginning to care for her, perhaps too much for his own good.

What if he got a call to do a piece about some rare object or some exotic place? What if he answered that call?

What if Paige had been right when she'd told him he'd never be able to give up his obsession with the camera?

What if he wouldn't be able to change, after all?

More to the point, was Laura really what he needed and wanted, or was he going through a rebound period triggered by his divorce?

Chapter Eight

Sam was startled out of his reverie when the kitchen door slammed and Laura appeared. Only this time, to his surprise, a different Laura.

Her signature white cotton man-tailored shirt was gone. In its place, she wore a sheer green-and-white-flowered blouse. Underneath the blouse, lush curves peeked through a white lacy bra. Her hair was brushed to one side, and a wisp flirted with her eyes. The worn jeans and sturdy boots she wore were a study in contradiction. But there was a glow about her.

Rather than looking like a fierce rancher defending her territory, Laura's softer appearance was decidedly eye-catching and feminine. Whatever had caused the change or whichever persona she'd intended to portray, she'd wound up looking like a mixture of feisty femininity and a warrior ready to take on the world.

He may have made a vow not to touch Laura, but sure as hell, he wanted to touch her now. He wanted to taste her lips, inhale her fresh scent and lose himself in her loveliness. He tore his gaze away from the vein throbbing in her slender neck. "Going somewhere?"

"Yes. I decided telephone calls are for the birds. I'm going into Montgomery to show the tax receipts to Pete."

Sam made a decision of his own. Considering the considerable change in her appearance, Laura would probably have men falling all over themselves after one good look. If she intended to go into town looking like a candy confection, he was going to go along to keep an eye on her. "Count me in," he said firmly. "I'd like to have a talk with Pete myself. Maybe get a better fix on what Hansen might be up to now."

"What makes you think he'd be stupid enough to try something else now?" She waved the packet of tax receipts in front of his nose. "I'm not coming back until the Lazy E's tax records are clean."

Sam nodded, but as far as he was concerned, Laura wasn't out of the woods yet. Not after he suspected the rumor about the legality of her adoption had Hansen's fingerprints all over it. "There's the rumor about your adoption, for one."

She peered at him suspiciously. "Has Pete told you something he hasn't told me?"

"No. Just a feeling." A feeling he couldn't explain, but one that had the hairs prickling on the back of his neck. He learned long ago not to ignore this feeling. It had kept him out of danger more than once.

"Then as far as I'm concerned, it's only a stupid rumor," Laura said firmly. "There was nothing wrong with my adoption. Dad told me and Mom he took care of everything."

"Probably," Sam said to placate her. Considering the bumpy road Laura's luck had taken for the past two years, he wasn't at all sure *probably* fit the bill. "I'll just go over to the county courthouse and ask around. Stay a step ahead of Hansen."

Laura's lips curled in disdain at the mention of Hansen. "You really think that man's behind the adoption rumor?"

"I could be wrong, but yes."

Laura shook her head, but from the frown that creased her forehead, Sam could see he'd set her thinking. Maybe that was a good thing—she'd be on her guard.

"Wouldn't hurt if I ask around," he added.

Laura dropped to the swing beside him. "Please don't. I'm afraid your questions would do more harm than good. I've lived around here for fifteen years, and I know there are more watchful eyes and listening ears in town than there are people.''

''Counting the sheep?'' He meant it as a joke, but the frown on Laura's forehead grew deeper.

''Very funny.'' Laura looked annoyed. ''I was only trying to warn you. Since Magraw spread the word about our living together, there's too much gossip about us out there already. Nosing around the county courthouse asking questions about my adoption isn't going to help.'' She was clearly agitated. Her blouse rose and fell with each breath she took.

Fascinated, Sam's body warmed and his thoughts turned to their too-brief encounter. If any other woman had dressed like this, he might have considered it an invitation.

He cleared his throat and forced his body to cool. ''That reminds me… About that scene back there in the bedroom, I—''

She blushed. ''You don't have to go there. I've already decided to forget it.''

The way she avoided meeting his gaze telegraphed that she remembered touching him and hadn't forgotten the way his lips had felt. If he hadn't promised not to touch her, he would have taken her in his arms and shown her how he felt. In detail. Although talking about what had taken place between them earlier clearly embarrassed her, he knew from the glow in her eyes that Laura didn't regret it any more than he did.

Even without the blush and her obvious discomfiture, Sam sensed that a woman like Laura didn't take sexual play lightly. And that if Laura ever decided to play, it would be for keeps.

He realized if all he'd meant was to tease Laura, he'd gone too far. Had he meant to tease, or had it been a desire to get closer to Laura?

Either way, the first prize for stupidity in teasing Laura belonged to him. "I'd still like to apologize."

Laura smiled ruefully and gazed earnestly into his eyes. "Don't. I didn't have to buy into your invitation, but the truth is, I couldn't help myself. I might not have asked for what happened earlier, but we're both old enough to know it takes two to tango."

Sam's interest was piqued. The longer she spoke, the more it seemed to him there was more to Laura's sensuality than was visible on the surface. She was right; sexual play required two willing players, and she'd said she'd been willing. Interesting, he thought, and an issue definitely worth pursuing. "So why did you kiss me?" he asked softly.

Laura blushed again. "Frankly, you're an attractive man, so I suppose it was a man-woman thing. Not that it's going to happen again. We hardly know each other," she added hurriedly when he started to break in. She took a deep breath. "So now that we understand each other, you don't have to think about it anymore." She rose. "I'm going into town."

Gently cradling Annie so as not to wake her, Sam got to his feet. Laura might have understood him, but he was darned if he understood her. "I'm still coming with you."

"Not without a car seat, you won't." She glanced meaningfully at the sleeping baby. "Maybe next time."

He was saved from a standoff when a large black luxurious car drove up and stopped, and a family of five spilled out. The man, obviously the father from the authoritarian way he directed traffic, was dressed in a dark-blue business suit, white shirt and maroon tie. The mother wore a beige linen suit and brown high heels. If it hadn't been for the three children scattering across the yard, Sam would have thought new potential buyers for the ranch had shown up.

Laura looked puzzled and headed for the visitors with Sam hard at her heels. "May I help you?"

"I'm Drake Abbott, and this is my wife, Jane," the man answered affably. "We came about the camp."

Laura smiled pleasantly. "Of course. I received your application the other day." She glanced over at the barn where the three Abbott children were transfixed with the little lamb Hank carried in his arms. "I'm sorry, I'm afraid you're early. Camp doesn't start until next week."

"I'm aware of that," Abbott said with a sidelong glance at his wife. "I'd tried to call you earlier, but for some reason I couldn't get through."

Laura bit her lower lip. Could there be a problem with her phone? Still, since the Abbotts appeared to take her acceptance for granted, she couldn't bring herself to send them home. Maybe it would be all right to accept the one child who'd been registered.

"Unfortunately I have to leave for London immediately, and my wife will be coming with me," Abbott went on. "I'm afraid we need to leave the children now."

"Children?" Laura frowned. She glanced over to where Hank had put the lamb on the ground. The animal was staggering around on its wobbly feet. The children were crouched in a circle, fascinated. "Your application was for only one child."

"True, for little Jacob," Jane Abbott replied with a light laugh clearly intended to dismiss Laura's concern. "At the time, Caitlin was too young, and Stanley wasn't interested. But that was before my husband had to report to London for a conference. I couldn't resist the opportunity to go with him." She smiled adoringly at her husband, gazed with approval at Sam, then turned back to Laura. "You do understand, don't you?"

Underneath that ladylike exterior, Laura sensed a character of steel. The woman wasn't prepared to take no for an answer.

Laura also understood she was also gazing at a woman determined not to allow her husband out of her sight, let alone see him fly alone six thousand miles away. After her own sensual moments with Sam, she understood Jane very well.

Now that Sam had managed to get under her skin the way he had, she was reluctant to think he might eventually go his way, just as Jane Abbott was reluctant to let her husband go overseas without her.

Laura glanced at Sam for support. He shrugged. The decision was clearly hers. With the added revenue she needed in mind, she asked, "how old are the other two children?"

"Caitlin is six, and Stanley is eleven." At Laura's frown, their mother hurried to add, "Don't worry, Stanley's old enough to help keep an eye on the other two."

Laura swallowed a sigh. If his doting mother thought a city-bred eleven-year-old could be a help on a sheep ranch, she was sadly mistaken. If the boy was anything like a typical eleven-year-old boy, Stanley would be one more child to keep an eye on. And if the kids were anything like their strong-minded mother, she was going to have her hands full.

When Laura didn't answer, Jane Abbott turned her gaze on Sam. "You do understand, don't you, Mr. Evans?"

Mr. Evans? Sam snapped to attention. He was tempted to set her straight, but there *was* Laura's reputation to think about. Now that it looked as if the camp was about to start earlier than expected, he had to play it cool. "Guess so," he answered. "Laura?"

She nodded reluctantly. "If you both will come up to the house, you can fill out and sign the application for Caitlin and her brother. Do the children have luggage?"

"In the trunk," Drake Abbott said, obviously relieved. "Jane, why don't you go on up and start filling out the applications? I'll get the suitcases out of the car and join you in a minute."

The man gazed after his wife and turned to Sam. "Women!"

Sam watched Laura sashay back to the house. Thank God she couldn't see or possibly know how his body stirred at the sight of her hips swaying under her tight jeans.

How had he ever thought Laura wasn't feminine?

He shrugged and waited until Laura was safely out of sight. "What would you have done if you'd been turned down?"

Abbott visibly shuddered. "Jane wouldn't have

taken no for an answer. Since you're a family man yourself, I knew I could count on you. And once I saw you with a kid of your own, I knew I had it made. I figured anyone who runs children's camps would understand the fix I'm in. Gotta like kids to run a children's camp, eh?''

Sam found himself nodding his agreement. Laura undeniably loved children. As for himself, outside of scouting, the closest he'd been around kids was when he was a kid himself. Unfortunately not a kid in this Abbott bunch could be considered a preteen Scout.

As for being called Mr. Evans, the idea of marriage with Laura was fascinating but a little frightening. Especially since his heart-to-heart with himself about where he wanted his relationship with Laura to go hadn't resolved much, if anything. Thank goodness there was still the camp to take his mind off more permanent matters. Besides, Annie seemed happy enough here. What was an extra day or two out of his life?

''Sorry I can't help you with the luggage,'' he told Drake Abbott when Annie stirred. ''My hands are full.''

''No bellhop?'' The man gazed at the mountain of luggage and the three tightly wrapped sleeping bags in the car's trunk.

''Not yet.'' Sam thought of the sheep-herder

friends of Hank's due to show up next week. He didn't know how old the two men were, but he sure hoped they were able to carry luggage. Otherwise it was undoubtedly going to be his job. He eyed the luggage speculatively. How heavy could a little kid's luggage actually be?

"What's with the sleeping bags?" he asked. "There are bunk beds upstairs for the kids."

Drake Abbott looked puzzled. "The list of supplies your wife sent calls for a sleep-out. Changed your mind?"

"No." Sam laughed. "With so much going on, guess I forgot."

The man sighed and reached for two suitcases. "Be back for the rest as soon as I sign those papers."

"Sure," Sam answered amiably. "I'll keep an eye on the car for you."

With the Abbott children occupied with checking out the bum lamb, Hank sauntered toward Sam. "Looks like the kids are here sooner than I figured," he muttered under his breath. "Guess we're in for it."

Sam shared Hank's misgivings. If Laura planned a sleep-out around a campfire, there was no telling what else she might have in mind. He'd better be prepared. "I don't know what Laura has planned for the camp when it opens. Any ideas to keep these three busy until then?''

Hank scratched his head. ''Kept a couple sheep out in back of the barn. I was going to teach the kids how to shear them. Maybe even prepare the wool for sale.''

Sam glanced over to where the poor little bum lamb was struggling to evade six hands and to stay on its feet. ''Sounds good. But what are you going to do with these three?''

''There's always the barn to clean up.''

''Good luck.'' Sam started to walk away. A thought struck him. ''By the way, try and keep the kids away from those old farm tools. Laura may need them.''

''Stuff ain't good for much. What's she going to do with 'em?''

''Ever hear of the *Antiques Road Show?*''

Hank thought for a moment. ''Nope. Can't say I have.''

''Take my word for it,'' Sam answered. ''The answer to Laura's money problems is rusting in the barn. Trouble is, after I told her what she thought was junk is actually valuable antiques, she wasn't too thrilled about selling.''

Hank eyed him with disapproval. ''Wouldn't think so. They belonged to Jonah, and his father before him.''

"Maybe so, but if push comes to shove, at least they're money in the bank."

Sam felt a pull on his trouser leg and looked down at Caitlin Abbott. "Is that your baby, mister?" The little girl's face lit up with interest as she gazed up at Annie. He nodded cautiously.

"Can I hold her?"

Sam studied the little girl. She wore boy's jeans, a Disneyland T-shirt, white socks and tennis shoes. Her blond hair was cut like a boy's, but there was no mistaking she was a little girl. He'd heard little girls liked babies, but this one was only six years old. Did he dare trust her to hold Annie?

He was about to beg off when a mental lightbulb lit up. If it was okay with Laura, allowing Caitlin to become involved with Annie's care was a sure way to keep the little girl happy and, better yet, busy. Seeing the way Laura took to little children, she was sure to agree.

After all, he was only doing what Laura had asked him to do—help with the campers. "I was just going up to the house to take care of the baby. Want to come along?"

Caitlin was so excited at the prospect of helping with Annie, she giggled, reached for Sam's hand and pulled him toward the house. "Can we go and do it right now?"

"Sure." A surge of emotion swept Sam at the

trusting way Caitlin gazed up at him. Her little hand in his brought a catch to his throat. If he had anything to do with it, Annie was going to look as innocent and happy as this when she grew older.

Annie stirred and awoke with a start. When her lips puckered and she looked ready to cry, Sam made for the house. "I'll take Caitlin here," he said to Hank. "You keep an eye on the other two, okay?"

"Sure." Hank looked over at the Abbott boys, but he didn't look too happy at the prospect.

Sam bit back a grin. "Laura told me *you* said little kids are like sheep. Tame one and the others will follow. Wasn't that what you said?"

"Yeah." Hank shrugged. "But that was before the kids showed up." His shoulders drooping, he headed back to the barn.

Sam grinned at Hank's back and, still holding Caitlin's hand, led her up to the house. "I'm kinda new at taking care of babies," he confessed, "but I guess between the two of us we ought to be able to do a pretty good job. Right?"

"Right!" Caitlin echoed. Her bright-blue eyes glittered with excitement as she danced along at his side. "I can help a lot, mister. I diaper real good. Susie—that's my doll—wets after I feed her."

"Since we're going to be working together, you can call me Sam," he offered, strangely at peace with himself and the world as he listened to the little girl's chatter. Maybe diapering a baby wasn't all that different from diapering a doll. At least, the principles ought to be the same.

He had to learn the good, the bad and the ugly of baby care sooner or later. As long he was lucky enough to be staying in a house with two maternity-ward nurses and now little Caitlin in residence to advise him, the sooner the better.

No sooner had they entered the house than Annie began to cry. Laura, deep in application forms, looked up.

In contrast with Jane Abbott's businesslike demeanor, Laura was the picture of femininity. Warm and very desirable.

Sam blinked and reminded himself there was a time and a place for everything. Unfortunately this wasn't the time and definitely not the place for what he had in mind. They both had a job to do, and he'd better get to his. "Annie just woke up."

Laura smiled. "She needs changing. She's probably hungry, too. There's a fresh bottle in the refrigerator."

Sam exchanged glances with Caitlin. "Ready?" The little girl nodded happily.

Her mother frowned. "Now, Caitlin, don't be a nuisance. Why don't you go outside and play with the boys?"

The smile vanished from the little girl's face as quickly as it had appeared. Sam bit his lip. "Caitlin's fine here with me," he said.

He began to wonder if her mother realized Caitlin *was* a little girl with all the feminine instincts nature had endowed her with. Or if Jane Abbot had been the one who had given Caitlin a doll. He put his hand on Caitlin's shoulder; he wasn't going to let her down. "We're going to be buddies."

Jane Abbott didn't look convinced. "Mrs. Evans?"

Laura's eyes softened as her gaze met Sam's. "Your daughter will be fine with Sam."

"Well, if you're sure. Just don't be a nuisance, Caitlin," Jane Abbott admonished again.

Sam picked up Annie's diaper bag and made for the kitchen. "Come on, Caitlin. Time for a lesson in how to diaper a baby."

Out of the corner of his eye, Sam saw Laura cover her mouth with her hand. He knew it was to keep from laughing, but hadn't he already told her that, biology aside, sometimes a man could be more nurturing than a woman? In his book, Jane Abbott, biological mother of three, was a prime example.

By the time he spread the changing pad on the kitchen table, Annie's tears had turned to wails. He murmured soothing words, handed her a pacifier and unsnapped her rompers. "How about handing me some wipes, Caitlin?"

Caitlin's eyes widened. "Wipes?"

Sam smiled to himself and reached for a blue plastic container of wipes. Under Caitlin's avid gaze, he removed Annie's damp diaper, gently wiped her off and applied a generous dose of talcum powder.

"Guess you don't use wipes and talcum powder when you change your Susie, do you?"

"Susie isn't a real baby," she whispered conspiratorially as if she was explaining a deep mystery. "I just pretend."

Sam nodded soberly and realized he didn't know much about babies or little girls. And the more he thought about the multifaceted Laura, he obviously didn't know much about grown women, either.

Chapter Nine

Laura began to worry when she realized she hadn't heard Sam's or Caitlin's voices for the past five minutes. Visions of Sam wrestling with a diaper and too proud to ask for help flashed through her mind. Even before she heard the sound of the Abbotts' car fade into the distance, she made for the kitchen.

Sam was seated holding his infant daughter in his arms. Annie sucked on her bottle with little mewing sounds of contentment. Caitlin, an enchanted smile on her face, was seated at Sam's feet gently stroking Annie's leg. Laura watched, fascinated, as Sam bent and kissed the baby's forehead.

The scene so much resembled a picture of a mother and children that Laura's heart skipped a beat. Only, in this case, the parent was a man. If she'd ever had doubts about the real man behind Sam's outward amiable persona, they faded now.

She was sure Sam was every bit the man he appeared to be: nurturing, caring and a man who loved children. And judging from the look on Caitlin's face, a man to whom children were drawn.

Sam may have professed ignorance of the care, feeding and other ways of children, but gazing at a contented Annie and a smiling Caitlin, she knew Sam didn't have to worry. The man was a natural.

A man who was a loving father had to have all the makings of becoming a loving husband, Laura thought as she watched the silent trio. Too bad Sam's ex-wife hadn't stuck around long enough to find that out. On the other hand, one woman's loss could be another woman's gain, she realized as she stood in the doorway gazing at a scene that touched her heart and soul.

Her gaze lingered on Sam. It wasn't only his nurturing side she admired, she thought. There was a lot more to the man than an instinctive gift for fatherhood. There was his reassuring presence, the warmth in his chocolate-brown eyes and the heart-stopping smile that seemed designed to break down a woman's defenses.

As she watched the trio, she made a silent vow. It was time to stop thinking of herself as less than a desirable woman. For the first time in her life, and maybe the last, she was going to stop worrying about propriety and act out a dream.

The next time Sam's eyes telegraphed a clear invitation, it wasn't going to be a game. She wasn't going to settle for just a touch, a fleeting kiss or a silent promise. He'd shown her the sensual woman hidden inside her. A woman who needed the right man to bring that part of her to the surface. In her heart of hearts, she sensed Sam could be that man.

True, she didn't believe in one-night stands or casual sex, but for once in her life she was going to do what her heart yearned for. And maybe, just maybe, Katy had been right when she told her Sam would love her enough to put away his walking boots.

The big problem was that she felt she owed Sam the truth before things went too far. She was barren. Once she told him the truth, what then? Would he stay?

The warm feeling around her heart slowly faded but not her desire. She would make love with Sam, she decided. But loving him had to be her secret.

She straightened her shoulders, cleared her throat and walked into the kitchen. "Looks as if you're going to have to move into another bedroom, Sam. Now that the Abbotts are here, they'll need the bunk beds."

"Not a problem." Sam tried not to show it, but he was tickled pink at having his fantasy of a bedroom next to Laura's room come true. "I'll get to it just as soon as Annie says enough."

"Your baby can talk?" Caitlin looked up at Annie with awe. "My baby just cries."

"Your baby?" Laura's knees seemed to turn to rubber. She looked to Sam for help, then in dismay at Caitlin. "Don't tell me there's another child in your family. Is he or she coming to camp, too?"

Sam grinned at Laura's look of dismay and decided to head for neutral territory. He shrugged and lifted Annie to his shoulder for the burping exercise Laura had recommended.

"Wait a minute!" Laura grabbed a cloth diaper and laid it on Sam's shoulder. "Just in case. Now, what's this about another baby?"

"Caitlin likes to pretend her doll, Susie, is a real baby," Sam explained. "Good training for the future, right?"

"Of course," Laura agreed, relieved that the Abbotts wouldn't return to leave another child in her care. "Maybe Caitlin can give you a few pointers."

"She already has," Sam said with a smile at Caitlin. "She's a heck of a helper, aren't you, sweetheart?"

The little girl dimpled. "I like babies. They're fun."

"Good," Laura said. "Then you can help me with Annie while Sam moves his things into another bedroom."

Sam handed Annie to Laura. "Which bedroom?"

"The bedroom next to mine." Laura buried her face in Annie's hair, but not before he saw her blush.

Sam held his breath. It had to be the same bedroom where he'd discovered the sensual woman lurking inside Laura. A woman he'd hoped to meet again. "The bedroom next to yours?"

"Yes." Laura's blush deepened. "There's a bathroom in between our bedrooms you're welcome to use. Of course," she added, "you'll have to remember to knock before you come in. Or if you'd rather, there's a small bathroom for the campers down the hall.

Sam envisioned standing in line while seven little campers took their time to shower and brush their teeth. The bathroom between Laura's bedroom and his won hands down. "No thanks," he said into Laura's blush. "I *will* remember to knock."

He charged upstairs, bundled his and Annie's things in his duffel bag and headed for his new quarters. On second thought, he took the bottom drawer out of the little chest of drawers and brought it with him into his new bedroom. Annie had to sleep somewhere, and in spite of Katy's offer, the somewhere was going to be with him.

But what if he'd been right about the message in Laura's eyes?

Not that he had anything to worry about, he thought as he caught himself. All Laura had offered him was a bedroom and access to a communal bathroom, nothing else. On the other hand, there *had* been the hint of an invitation in her eyes.

One day at a time, he told himself as he looked around the bedroom for a good place to put the dresser drawer. No matter how much he wanted to respond to Laura's invitation, he had to take things one day at a time.

He came downstairs in time to see Hank walking up the steps to the front door carrying a beautifully carved cradle. He strolled out to meet him. "Where did the cradle come from?"

"Found it buried back in a corner of the barn when the boys and I were straightening up. Thought you might want to use it for Annie." Hank reached into his back pocket for a bandanna and surveyed the cradle with a critical eye. "There's spiderwebs and a little dust—nothing a good cleaning won't take care of."

Sam gingerly rocked the cradle with the toe of his boot. "Whose cradle was it?"

"For the kids Elsie couldn't have." Hank bent and began to dust the cradle. He delved into every corner of the intricately carved headboard as gently as if it had been made of glass. Sam hunkered down beside him to take a closer look. "Does Laura know about the cradle?"

"Nope. Jonah told me he was going to surprise

Elsie with it when the time came—only, the time never came. Once they decided to adopt an older kid, Jonah told me to give the cradle away. Couldn't do it. Not after I'd seen him carve it out behind the barn so that Elsie wouldn't see.''

Sam regarded the small piece of furniture. It didn't take much imagination to envision the love that had been carved into each spindle and the angels on the headboard. Or the heartbreak that had eventually led Jonah to tell Hank to give the cradle away.

What was clear, Sam thought as he gazed at the expression on Hank's face, was that his little heartbreaker daughter had captured another heart.

''I'd be proud to use it for Annie as long as we're here.'' Sam reached to dust off a spot Hank had missed.

''Going somewhere?'' Hank sat back on his heels and peered at Sam.

''Sooner or later,'' Sam replied. ''But not before I see to getting someone to put up a new water tower. Which reminds me, how are you doing with the fence?''

''Patched it for now. Saving the real job for the boys.''

''The Abbott boys?'' Sam's pride was hurt. If he wasn't the man to help repair the fence, what could the youngsters do for Hank? "They're a little young for the job, don't you think?"

"Heck no. I was talking about Al and Jim," Hank answered with a final flourish of the bandanna. "Goin' to do it right this time. When we get through, the fence will last another hundred years." He peered at Sam. "Providing another city slicker doesn't take it out."

Sam bit back a laugh. The "boys" were no doubt the same age as Hank—in their sixties or seventies. "I'll remember that," he answered.

Hank nodded and abruptly changed the subject. He glanced around, then lowered his voice. "Katy says you're taken with Laura. She right?"

"Could be. Laura's a great woman," Sam replied. He sensed it wasn't like Hank to get personal. The man apparently believed the less said the better.

Hank regarded him under raised eyebrows. "That all?"

Sam shrugged. "I still have some photography assignments I'm committed to. And there's Annie to think of."

Hank dusted the cradle gliders, stood and stuffed the bandanna in his back pocket. "Guess a man's gotta do what he's gotta do. As long as you don't hurt Laura." He gestured to the snowcapped mountains in the distance. "Ought to be plenty to photograph right around here."

Sam looked him squarely in the eye. "Don't worry. I'm not leaving just yet, and I'd never do anything to hurt Laura. I promised her I'd stay and help with the camp for a while."

Hank nodded and turned to leave.

"Hey, wait a minute!" Sam motioned to the cradle. "Aren't you going to tell Laura about finding the cradle in the barn?"

Hank looked back over his shoulder. "Nope. Figure it's your job to tell her. Gotta get back to the barn. Left those two kids going through the place like there's a pot of gold hidden in there somewhere."

"My job?" Judging from the sparkle in Hank's eyes, Sam sensed the man was trying to tell him something. A something Katy had also mentioned. Either Hank and Katy had been comparing notes about their obvious growing attraction or he'd given away the way he was beginning to feel about Laura.

Sam gazed after Hank until he disappeared into the barn. The wily old man, usually so spare with words, had set him thinking. And not only about Laura. It was time to start making plans for the future.

He gazed down at the beautifully carved cradle. It might have been carved out of cherry wood, but in Jonah Evans's mind, the cradle he'd lovingly carved so many years ago had been more precious than gold.

And now that he thought about it, so was Laura.

He picked up the cradle and headed into the house to show it to Laura. But not before he braced himself for what had to come next.

Laura was settling a sleepy Annie on a blanket in front of the fireplace. She looked up at his entrance. "What a beautiful cradle! Where did you get it?"

"Hank found it in the barn."

Laura frowned. "I don't remember ever having seen it there. Are you sure?"

"I'm sure." Sam set the cradle on the floor and thought fast. He hated to tell Laura the true story behind the cradle. The last thing he wanted to do was break her heart. Since he had to say something, he made up a story sure to please her. "Hank told me he saw your father carving the cradle years ago. Maybe he intended it for the children you would have someday."

To his surprise, instead of looking pleased, Laura's face paled. For a moment he thought she might faint. He took a cautious step toward her and held out his hand. "Are you okay?"

She took a deep breath. "Sam, we have to talk."

In an effort to break the tension that suddenly seemed to blanket the room, Sam laughed nervously. "Hey, that's my line. I thought we already did."

"No," she answered with a quick glance to where Caitlin was playing with Annie. "I'm serious. We have to talk."

Sam didn't know what to think. After their frank talk in the bedroom about how it took two to tango, what was there left to say?

He was saved from asking the question when there was a knock on the door and the sheriff walked in without waiting for an answer. "Got a minute, Laura?"

Laura bit her lower lip and slowly got to her feet. "Later," she told Sam under her breath. She'd intended to tell him the cradle would never be used for her children because she could never have any. He looked uncertain, but he nodded.

With a last yearning glance at the cradle, Laura sighed and turned to the sheriff. "I was planning to go to town to talk to you today. I wanted to show you the tax receipts we found before I put them in the bank. What's up?"

Pete hesitated. "You might want to have this conversation in private."

"Why? Sam already knows everything there is to know about the tax receipts."

Pete cleared his throat. "This isn't about property taxes, Laura."

For the second time in the past few moments, Laura felt a chill. The grim expression on Pete's face was a dead giveaway. Whatever news he brought this time wasn't going to be any better than the last time. She motioned Sam to stay. "What *is* it about?"

Pete cleared his throat and looked as if he wished he was anyplace but here. "That dang-fool rumor about your adoption that's going around town."

Laura wrapped her arms around herself. The brief hope she'd had that nothing else could possibly go wrong faded in a heartbeat. "Have you found out who started the rumor?"

"No, sorry to say. I'm afraid the rumor is louder than ever." Pete said grimly. "The dang thing seems to be feeding on itself. Someone's going to have to look into it before things get out of hand."

"I don't understand, Pete," Laura said. "Why would anyone start a rumor like that now? I was adopted more than fifteen years ago."

Pete cast a telling look at Sam before he turned back to Laura. "Hard to tell. Maybe to make you so uncomfortable you'd be ready to sell out?"

Sam realized the sheriff, in his own way, was trying to tell him something. Was the talk about Sam's presence on the ranch and the latest rumor about Laura designed to embarrass her deeply enough to get her to sell the ranch? If so, Magraw or Hansen had to be the bastards who started the rumors. And why couldn't Pete do something about it?

"That doesn't make sense," Laura said before Sam could intervene. The more she thought about the rumor, the angrier she grew. She'd defend her right to the ranch with a rifle that could shoot, if necessary. "Everyone who's known me all these years couldn't possibly care if I was adopted legally or not."

"You're right, but it's not only the people who know you who are talking." Pete shrugged helplessly, hesitated then went on, "It's not just those fool rumors that worry me. It's what some people might do about it."

Some people? Sam couldn't keep silent any longer. From the tone in the sheriff's voice, the missing tax receipts and the rumors, including the one about his shacking up with Laura, had to be only the tip of the iceberg. "Just what do you think people might do, Sheriff?"

Pete rolled his hat between his fingers and regarded Sam silently. To Sam's way of thinking, the reason the sheriff was reluctant to answer had to have as much to do with Laura as with her unknown nemesis.

"You may as well spit it out, Pete," Sam finally prompted. "Whatever's worrying you might get out of hand if you don't."

"To tell you the truth, I *was* thinking of something more violent than rumors." Pete glanced meaningfully at Laura. "I don't want anyone to get hurt."

"Are you saying Laura might go after Hansen or whoever with a gun?" Incredulous, Sam couldn't keep the skepticism out of his voice. Laura may have been carrying a rifle the first time they met, but the idea she might use it blew his mind. Certainly not the Laura he knew. Behind him he heard Laura gasp.

Pete sent Laura a warning look. "It's a possibility. Or just maybe this could be someone else's turn with a weapon."

"All for a piece of real estate?"

"Yep. Some people do a lot worse than spread malicious rumors to get what they want."

Laura had had enough. "You don't have to worry about me, Pete. As far as I'm concerned, since no one else has offered to buy the ranch, that leaves Hansen. Are you saying he might be behind all this?"

"Don't know and don't think you have time to find out." This time Pete gazed pointedly at Sam. "If you really want to help Laura, you're going to have to put out the fires, one at a time. Starting now."

"I do and I will," Sam replied, never more serious in his life. If Laura needed protection from

Hansen, or from herself, he was her man. "You have my word on it."

"In that case," Pete went on, "my advice for you is to get yourselves a copy of that adoption certificate mighty soon."

Sam nodded soberly. With Pete directing his comments to him, it appeared Pete believed he and Laura were a twosome. If not now, then sometime in the future. To his surprise, the longer he thought about the prospect, the more Sam began to find the idea inviting. Any future plans he might have had for himself had to wait. He was Laura's for the duration.

He looked at her. After the way she'd taken him and Annie in, how could anyone, including him, have thought she was the type to willingly harm someone?

"How about I visit the county courthouse," Sam suggested, "check through adoption records and see what I can find."

Laura shook her head. "If what Pete says is true about the gossip that we are a twosome, then we have to talk."

Since he didn't know what Laura had in mind for that talk, Sam gave up the idea of trying to convince her. He'd listen to Pete's advice—take one day at a time and one problem at a time. If all went as he hoped, he and Laura would have plenty of time to talk later. "Okay. If you'll keep an eye on Annie for me, I'll hitch a ride into town with Pete."

"Sorry," Pete said. "The courthouse closes at noon on Friday. With Monday being a holiday, guess you'll have to wait until Tuesday."

Sam met Laura's concerned gaze and silently prayed nothing else went wrong before Tuesday.

Chapter Ten

The scent of Laura's aromatic body wash was finally Sam's undoing.

The green plastic container resting on the edge of the bathtub not only promised sensual bliss, but also the nude figure on the label didn't help to keep his thoughts pure. And certainly not when he inhaled the spicy scent and imagined the figure as Laura.

One thing was clear: he and Laura had to come to an understanding. Her lips may have said hands off, but her eyes made him yearn for the taste of those lips. Better yet, her body curled into his as he made love to her.

He'd tried to keep busy to avoid thinking about Laura and her growing hold on his life.

He'd spent the past two days helping Laura and Katy get another bedroom ready for the campers. But all he could think about was Laura's bedroom next to his.

Over Hank's protests, Sam had pitched in and helped Hank and his two elderly friends replace the wooden fence separating the Lazy E from the county road. He hadn't thought of Laura for eight hours and had the splinters to prove it.

Remembering his collision with the water tower, he'd called and left a message with a local construction company to come out and replace the water tower as soon as possible.

In short, he'd done everything he could to keep busy. Outside of helping in the kitchen, he'd run out of things to do.

Nothing seemed to take his mind off her.

He dried off after a long hot shower, inhaled the sweet, almost spicy scent of Laura's body wash and mulled over her magical transformation from a hard-nosed rifle-toting defender of her territory into a sexy and desirable woman.

What he should have been thinking about was his mother's favorite admonition that the road to hell was paved with good intentions. In this case, surely hell was a sweet beautiful woman whose clear green eyes asked questions he couldn't answer.

It wasn't going to be easy. Not with the tantalizing scent of that body wash drifting through the bathroom door. And the knowledge that her bedroom was just beyond.

Thoughts, each one more sensual than its predecessor, spilled through his mind. His body stirred at the memory of the invitation he'd seen dawning in Laura's eyes—before Pete had shown up to turn her smile into a frown.

There was one thing he *was* sure of. Laura had done more than get under his skin like an itch he couldn't reach. The speed with which she'd managed to worm her way into his heart was almost frightening. Hadn't he told himself after his divorce that he had many more mountains to cross and many more pictures to take? Settling down again would have been the farthest thing from his mind—if he hadn't already lost his mind.

One way or another, he intended to get to the talk Laura wanted because he was sure it wasn't about the gossip. Tonight, if possible. After she was done talking, it was going to be his turn. And this time, he wasn't going to make a fool's promise not to touch her. Or to keep his hands planted behind him while she touched him.

The next time they were alone, his hands were going to be firmly planted on Laura's waist while he kissed her speechless. And if events went as he hoped, he intended to cash in on the promise he'd seen in her eyes earlier. This time, he was going to give himself a break.

He glanced through the bathroom window. Thank goodness the sky was clear and the spring rains had come and gone. He'd had enough of Colorado rain and unmarked muddy roads to last him a lifetime. On the other hand, he mused wryly, maybe he ought to be grateful to Mother Nature for the storm that had played a major part in his meeting Laura.

He hung up the damp towel and headed back to his bedroom to get ready for what Laura had dubbed a trial run sleep-out around a campfire.

The grime of fence-building washed away, he pulled on a fresh pair of jeans, a checkered green-and-white shirt and his boots, which this time he'd cleaned himself. With only three little campers to keep a wary eye on, sleeping out under the stars had to be a cinch. Sleeping across a campfire from Laura would not; he'd think of it as a test.

Dusk was falling by the time he grabbed a heavy denim jacket, Annie's little fleece sleeper, a couple of extra diapers and headed for the back porch, where Hank had set up headquarters.

The Abbott children each clutched a sleeping bag. Katy, with Annie strapped to her in some kind of backpack was checking the supplies. Fancy, his eyes warily eyeing the older Abbott boy, crouched at her feet. Hank and his two friends had custody of several boxes brimming with supplies. The only thing missing was a warm breeze and a full moon.

The children's expectant faces made him ashamed of his own lack of enthusiasm. Sleeping on the ground around a campfire had been exciting when he'd been fifteen. It didn't sound as much fun now that he was a six-foot-two-inch 180-pound man.

Thank God he didn't have to worry about Annie. His infant daughter seemed happy enough no matter where she was or whom she was with as long as she was dry and fed.

He glanced around for the person in charge. "Where's Laura?"

Hank shrugged, looked disgusted and gestured over his shoulder. "Headed into the barn for an old iron pot. Said no campfire cookout worth its salt would be the same without it."

Sam gazed at what he considered was already a mountain of supplies. There had to be enough pots and pans in the boxes for an entire Scout troop, let alone for nine people. Ten counting Annie. "What's so special about an old iron pot?"

Hank glared at the barn. "Jonah used to hang it over the campfire to bake beans. Should have known this was going to happen."

"That's because Laura's a sentimental woman," Katy retorted. "She's trying to recreate the campfires her father used to make when she was little. To hear her tell it, the beans were sheer ambrosia, made with bacon and the best honey. Not just any old beans."

"Yeah, and next she's going to want to grill steak

and roast potatoes under hot charcoal embers. What kind of cookout do you call that?''

"Laura's kind, old man.''

Al, who obviously didn't have the sense to keep quiet, broke in. "Ain't anything like the grub we used to have.'' He smacked his lips. "I can taste them beans already.''

Katy sniffed. "Well, you eat the beans. We're going to have steak and roasted potatoes.'' Al clamped his lips shut, but the look in his eyes matched Katy's.

"I think I'll go see if Laura needs help,'' Sam said hastily. There seemed to be more going on here than the merits of steak versus baked beans, and he had more important things on his mind. He headed for the barn and peered through the darkness.

"Laura?''

A faint moan answered him. Alarmed, he slowly made his way through the darkness. "Where are you? And what in blazes are you doing in here without a light?''

"Hang on a minute,'' she called out. "There's a flashlight around here somewhere. I dropped it when I tripped.''

Laura's voice was faint enough to make Sam's heart start to pound. Before he could panic, the flashlight came on, and he saw Laura sprawled on the floor.

Muttering a curse, Sam rushed over to help her sit up. "What happened? Are you okay?"

"I think so," she answered. "If you give me a minute, I'm sure I'll be fine."

From the shaky sound of her voice, Sam wasn't convinced. "What hurts?"

"My ankle."

"Do you mind if I check you over?"

When he touched the ankle, she gasped. "I must have banged it when I tripped over the hoe."

"Woman, I think you've messed yourself up some," he said. "Of all the fool things to do, coming in here in the dark has to be the dumbest. With all the junk scattered around here, you could have really hurt yourself!"

"I'm an idiot," she agreed. "I thought I knew just where to find what I was looking for. Someone must have moved things around."

"Probably the Abbott boys." Sam made a mental note to have a heart-to-heart with the kids and impress them with the fact that there was no gold in the barn. "Hank told me they were in here looking for gold yesterday."

"Gold? In the barn?" Laura struggled to sit up and straighten out her foot. "You've got to be kidding. Where could they have gotten such a wild idea?"

Sam thought of Hank's comment that Jonah Evans

had treated the cradle as if it had been made of gold. "Yeah, well, it's a long story, but I don't think you'd be interested." He got to his feet. "Come on, I'll help you up. Everyone's ready to get started."

She grabbed his hand, struggled to rise, and then fell back. "Sorry, I'm afraid I'm not going anywhere. I must have sprained my ankle." She peered around her. "Maybe you can use a wheelbarrow to get me out of here."

Sam bit back a burst of laughter at the idea of wheeling Laura back to the house like a load of hay. Then he had a better idea.

"Forget the wheelbarrow," he said. "Here, put an arm around my neck and try to keep the flashlight shining in front of me." Before she could protest, he lifted her into his arms and strode to the barn door.

"Please don't make a big deal out of this," Laura whispered. "I don't want everyone to worry. Or call off the sleep-out."

Sam caught his breath. Since it was clear Laura was in pain, someone was going to have to stay with her tonight. It had to be him, since the Abbott kids might need Katy's medical attention. The grin-and-bear-it attentions of three old men who lived in the past wouldn't cut it.

As soon as Katy spotted him coming out of the

barn with Laura in his arms, she rushed over. "Laura, honey, what on earth happened?"

Laura lifted her head from Sam's shoulder. "I must have sprained my ankle when I tripped over a hoe," she said.

Hank, with the Abbott kids hard at his heels, came running up. "Let me give you a hand." He put out his arms to take Laura.

Sam sidestepped him and held Laura closer. "No thanks. I'm taking her up to the house." He stopped in midstride and looked back. "I'm afraid Laura's not going to be able to go anywhere tonight."

Katy shrugged out of the harness that held Annie. "I'll come with you. I want to take a look at that ankle. Here, Hank. You keep an eye on Annie."

Annie, by now obviously used to being passed around like a basketball, burbled happily and reached for Hank's mustache. Hank's eyes widened. "What am I supposed to do with her?"

"Watch her until I come back," Katy said over her shoulder. "She won't bite."

"I can help you watch Annie," Caitlin offered shyly. "I'm good at helping with babies."

Hank eyed the baby warily. "That's good. I'm not."

"Can't be much different than taking care of a baby lamb," Jim offered. "Fix a bottle of milk and feed her."

Hank shuddered. "That'll be the day," he muttered as he glared at the door that closed behind Katy. "I'm taking the kid back to the house. This is a job for a grown woman."

Trailed by Katy, Sam carried Laura into her bedroom and gently set her down on the bed. "Are you going to be okay?"

Laura nodded. She wasn't about to tell Sam she'd been thinking about sleeping beside him in front of a campfire when she'd tripped over the hoe. Sleeping near enough to feel as though they were spending the night together, yet far enough away to stay out of trouble.

Now she gazed up into Sam's concerned brown eyes and wondered if she really wanted to stay out of trouble. Pass up a chance to make a dream come to life?

The answer was no; she had to face the truth. She wanted Sam in the way a woman wants a man she cares for. She'd waited long enough for this man, and she didn't intend to let the night pass without him. "There's no use in disappointing the campers, Katy. You go on. With Sam's help, I'll be fine."

Hank appeared in the doorway. "No way is this kid going to spend the night out in the open without you and Sam there to keep an eye on her. Katy's going to have her hands full with those two boys."

Sam sighed at the thought of what parents must

go through to find some quality time alone. "Don't worry, Katy. I'll take good care of Annie."

Katy didn't look convinced, but she handed Annie over. "If that's what you and Laura want. I'll bring up an ice pack to put on that ankle before I leave."

Sam swallowed a sigh of relief. With Katy out of the way, Annie asleep next door and Laura unable to walk, this could be a good time to get that talk Laura wanted out of the way. Once it was, they could move on to more important matters.

He waited impatiently while Laura tried to make herself comfortable and until Katy returned with a bag of ice cubes wrapped in a kitchen towel.

"Be sure and change the ice pack every few hours. And give Laura two of these every four hours if she needs them." She handed Sam a bottle of over-the-counter pain relievers. "I gave Annie her bottle an hour ago, so she'll probably fall asleep any minute."

From the doubtful way Katy eyed him, it was clear she wasn't sure he was capable of caring for Annie. Or Laura. It was up to him to prove her wrong on both counts. He turned back to Laura when Katy left. "Mind waiting while I take Annie next door and put her to bed?"

"I'm not going anywhere," Laura answered with a smile. "Are you sure you can handle the baby by yourself?"

"No problem," he answered confidently. "A diaper change was lesson number one, remember?"

Laura remembered a lot of things about Sam, some of them touching and heartwarming like changing a diaper. And a number of things about him that stirred all of her senses. The sensual look in his eyes when he thought she wasn't looking was number one.

She was sitting on the bed with her leg propped up on a pillow when Sam returned. "Annie fell asleep as soon as her head hit the pillow."

He eyed Laura's boots and form-fitting jeans. "Guess you're going to have to take off those boots if the cold pack is going to do your ankle any good."

She looked at him helplessly. "I've already tried while you were gone, but it hurts too much." She gestured to her jeans. "I guess I'll have to take these off, too. Any ideas?"

Sam swallowed hard. *Did he have any ideas? That had to be the question of the year.*

"Look here, Laura," he hedged when his conscience spoke to him. Taking advantage of an injured woman was definitely a no-no. "Considering the circumstances, do you have any idea what you're asking me to do?"

"I think so," she said. A mischievous smile lit up her eyes. "Do you?"

Sam wrestled with his conscience. He might have been mistaken the first time he'd thought he'd seen an invitation in her eyes, but he sure couldn't mistake the invitation he saw now.

"I think so," he echoed. He swallowed hard and lifted Laura's feet over the edge of the bed until she was in a sitting position. That accomplished, he knelt at her feet, gently eased the boot off her good foot and stopped to consider his next move. No way was he going to get the boot off her injured ankle without hurting her.

"Hang on a minute." Sam reached into his back pocket for the small Swiss Army knife he always kept with him just in case. "This might hurt a little, but I'll try to take it as easy as I can."

He gently lifted her foot, propped it up against his knee while he gingerly cut through the soft leather.

"Now my jeans, please."

Sam took a deep breath. Helping Laura off with her jeans would be tempting a saint, and at the moment he sure didn't feel saintly. "Are you sure you can't handle doing it yourself?"

She made a show of testing her ankle by pressing her foot against his knee and winced again. "I don't think so."

"Wait a minute," he said. "Before I start, I think this calls for an aspirin or two."

He headed into the bathroom, poured a glass of

water and hurried back. "Here," he said. "Better take these. If we get into a wrestling match, at least it won't hurt so much."

She swallowed the pills and took a deep breath. "I'm ready. Go ahead."

Sam was ready, too. And not just to remove the remaining boot. He wanted to take Laura in his arms and show her just how ready he was. First he had to make sure he was getting the right signals.

"Are you sure you don't want to have that talk first?"

She smiled and that invitation came into her eyes again. "Somehow talking doesn't seem important anymore."

"Why not?" he asked cautiously. No way did he intend to take advantage of an injured woman.

She shrugged and smiled. "It doesn't matter. Right now I need to have my jeans off so you can put that cold pack on my ankle before the ice melts."

"I'm game if you are," he answered. The room seemed to grow warm when she unbuckled her belt and tackled the zipper. He muttered to himself, put his hands around her waist and gently tugged her jeans down her slender hips.

It was then he discovered Laura's favorite color had to be pink. Sam got a good look at the limbs that put the woman on the body-wash label to shame.

He forced himself to remember he was here to take care of Laura, not to take an inventory of her charms.

He pulled back the quilt and helped her into bed. "You'll do for now." He tucked a pillow under her injured ankle, placed the ice pack on top of it and then covered her with the quilt. But not before he imagined himself lying there beside her.

"Looks as if it's going to be a long night," he said grimly. "Any ideas to pass the time?"

"A few," she said with a soft smile that sent Sam's good intentions out of his mind. "That is, if you're up to it."

"If *I'm* up to it?" Sam bit back a laugh. "If you only knew."

"Why don't you show me?" Laura's wicked smile made his bones turn to jelly.

Gazing at her full tempting lips, Sam realized Laura had changed more than her outward appearance. Somewhere in the past few hours, she'd not only changed her personality, but also turned into a sensuous and desirable woman. And, to his mounting delight, was honest enough to show it.

Was she really inviting him? he wondered. Or was it because he wanted her so? Gazing at the sparkle in her eyes, he saw the answer. She was inviting him.

He stretched out alongside her on the bed. "I figure the least I can do is keep you company, right?"

Dimples danced across Laura's cheeks. He took that as a yes. The closer he got to her, the closer he wanted to be. He put his arms around her. Laura smiled and settled against his shoulder. Good enough for now, he thought. "I wouldn't want to do anything to hurt you," he said softly.

"It's only my ankle that's in trouble," she answered, and nestled closer.

"Only your ankle?" he asked, knowing he was playing with fire. If he had his way, it was a fire that could consume them both.

She pulled away and sat up. "The rest of me seems to be in good shape."

"You bet it is." He reached for the pink buttons on her blouse and parted them one by one. With each button undone, he bent to kiss the sweet hollow between her breasts.

Her fingers traced his face, his brow, his lips. Every tender touch built a spiral of desire in him. He might have been down this road before, but never like this. And certainly never with a woman as generous and giving as Laura.

"Very good shape," he murmured. He reached behind her back, unhooked her bra, and slowly ran a gentle finger down her cheek. After a deep kiss that promised more, he moved his lips down her slender neck to her breasts.

When Sam tasted her sensitive breasts, Laura caught her breath. She pressed his head closer and knew, just as she'd known for the past twenty-four hours, that Sam was the man she'd been waiting for all her life. He was the right man, and it was the right time to fulfill the womanly need in her she'd denied herself too long.

As for whatever tomorrow might bring, tonight was the time for her to enjoy being a new woman.

She pulled away. "Let me," she whispered when Sam murmured his protest. "I'm not going anywhere. I just want to get into something more comfortable."

"Something more comfortable?" he said incredulously. His body began to ache, and his jeans grew tight at the thought of what Laura seemed to suggest. "What could be more comfortable than this?" He motioned to her unbuttoned blouse.

"If you'll let me go for a minute, I'll show you." She drew her blouse over her head and tossed it to the foot of the bed.

Sam's lips burned to move over her silky skin. Only this time, he wouldn't stop at touching. The old Laura was gone. This new Laura, a woman who took pride in being a woman, took his breath away. "You're sure about this?"

"Yes," she answered boldly. She settled back against the pillows with that tantalizing invitation back in her eyes. "Just as long as you don't have a wrestling match in mind."

"Hardly." He loved her smile, the invitation in her voice, the magic in her eyes. Visions of loving her raced through his mind. He would kiss every inch of her until they were both lost in a sensual haze. Tender loving would surely do the rest.

"Come closer," she whispered, and reached for the top button of his shirt. With her tongue caught between her teeth, she undid the buttons one by one.

By the time she'd reached his belt buckle and undid it and then the zipper, Sam ached to catch her tongue between his lips, to taste the honey of her mouth. Now it was his turn to move away. "Let me."

He stood and removed the rest of his clothing, his gaze locked with hers. "With a little cooperation and a big dose of ingenuity, maybe between the two of us we can blaze a few new trails where your ankle won't hurt."

She laughed happily, then almost forgot to breathe when he reached into his wallet for a small foiled-wrapped package.

Sam froze at the look that came over her face.

"Something wrong? Is it your ankle?" She shook her head. "You haven't changed your mind?"

She released her breath, shook her head and held out her arms. This was no time to tell Sam she didn't believe in one-night stands. Nor the time to tell him he didn't have to worry about getting her pregnant. She wanted to feel him inside her, to taste him, to touch him. To hear his throaty voice murmur in her ear.

"Sweetheart, for a minute you had me worried," he joked, but she heard the relief in his voice.

She thrust her errant thoughts away and held out her hands to take him to her. "You haven't changed *your* mind, have you?"

He hurriedly sheathed himself and rejoined her on the bed. "Don't even think about it."

When Sam's mouth descended on hers, her body burst into flame. When he kissed the palm of her hand and the inside of her wrist, then kissed his way up her arm to her elbow, she listened to her heart's desire. Aware only of Sam's hard heated lips on her skin and his hard body pressed to hers, she turned into his welcoming arms.

"Someday we're going to have to have that talk you wanted, but not tonight," he whispered. "Tonight we have only this." The last thing he heard before he lost himself in Laura's warmth was her soft "I love you."

Chapter Eleven

Sam remained awake long after Laura had fallen asleep in his arms. The sound of her voice murmuring, ''I love you,'' still echoed in his ears. Words spoken in the throes of sexual release, but deep inside, Sam knew Laura wouldn't have said she loved him if she hadn't meant it.

He gently brushed his thumbs across the silky skin of her shoulder and lost himself in the possibility of a future with this woman. There was no doubt in his mind he cared for her, but the idea she might actually be in love with him left him with a hollow feeling in the pit of his stomach. If Paige had told him he'd been a failure as a husband, what made him think he could do any better with Laura?

Considering the way he felt about entering another relationship after his traumatic divorce, loving Laura tonight had to be a mistake. Maybe not a mistake, he mused wryly as he inhaled Laura's scent

and his body responded to the feel of her silken skin
against his. Not a mistake, considering the sensual
night just passed, but definitely not wise.

Laura had been a challenge from the first moment
he'd seen her coming at him hell-bent for leather.
The change from a rifle-toting spitfire into a tender
loving woman had triggered a response in him that
defied reason. Yesterday's unspoken invitation had
taken him by surprise. But, invitation or not, he
should have recognized the warning signals that she
was falling in love with him long before he heard
her say, "I love you."

That was the rub.

He wasn't sure he wanted Laura to love him. Not
now, not until he came to grips with who he was,
where he was going and what he wanted out of life.
He hadn't known the answers when he'd been married to Paige, and he didn't know them now. They
were lessons he still had to learn before he made
any commitments.

Besides, there was Annie to think of.

How could he have not seen Laura was falling in
love with him? How could he have traveled so far
down a path he'd sworn never to travel again so
soon after his divorce?

Laura deserved a man who was ready to make a
commitment, and he wasn't that man. At least not

yet. Until he was, all he would accomplish by hanging around was to break her heart.

He glanced at the digital clock beside the bed. It read 6 a.m. Shafts from the rising sun began to shine through the bedroom curtains. Annie would soon be awake, and Katy and the campers would be coming back. The last place he wanted to be found was in bed with Laura.

He kissed the top of Laura's head, gently eased out of her arms and tucked the quilt around her. Gathering his clothing, he stopped and looked back. He wanted Laura again, this passionate direct woman who in the short time he'd known her had managed to mean so much to him. Asleep, she looked like an angel, but he knew better. Last night in his arms she'd been all woman, unabashedly wanton and eager. In her arms he'd reached sensual heights he'd never known before.

The memory of his heated response almost brought him back to her side. He hesitated in the doorway before he forced himself to turn away. As soon as he'd cleaned up, he'd take Annie, go downstairs and start up a pot of strong coffee and try to put his head on straight.

Fresh towels had been laid out for his use, but the rumpled towel Laura had used last night was the one that drew him. He buried his face in her spicy scent and thought of what could have been if this were another time and place.

Since he was fifteen, he'd dreamed of becoming a happily married man. Of creating a family like the one he'd lost when his father died. He thought his chance had come with Paige, but somewhere along the line that dream had blown up in his face. He hadn't been blameless, but then, a man couldn't stay where he wasn't wanted. He'd lost a wife, but at least he had his child.

He carefully folded the towel and headed for his bedroom where Annie still slept soundly in the cradle. One thing for sure, he was getting in too deep too fast. If he hadn't promised to help Laura settle her inheritance once and for all, he would have taken Annie and moved on.

THE SOUND of the bathroom door closing woke Laura. Disoriented at finding herself alone and undressed, she turned on to her back and glanced around the bedroom. The last thing she remembered was curling spoon-style into Sam's warmth, his arms around her. She smiled at the memory.

Sam had proved a gentle lover and, true to his promise, an innovative one. Together they'd blazed trails she'd never thought to travel. The thought that she and Sam would take up again where they'd left off when he came back to bed brought another, deeper smile to her face.

Several minutes went by before she finally realized Sam wasn't coming back to bed. If there hadn't been an indentation on the pillow beside her and the still warm sheet to remind her she'd spent the night in his arms, she would have thought it had been a dream.

Tentatively she wiggled the toes on her injured ankle. So far, so good. A night of loving appeared to have been a surefire cure for a sprained ankle.

The sound of voices downstairs in the kitchen brought her out of bed. Favoring her ankle, she pulled on her jeans and an old sweatshirt, her favorite slippers, and gingerly made her way downstairs.

The Abbott children were gathered around the kitchen table where Katy was pouring hot chocolate. Annie was sucking away on her bottle. Sam, Hank, Al and Jim were standing around drinking coffee. A mound of eggs and a slab of bacon waited beside the stove.

"Coffee, Laura?" Sam reached behind him for another cup. "Cream and sugar?"

Laura nodded and hobbled over to the table. Sam's polite and distant manner left her uncertain. The warmth in her middle was replaced by a cold feeling. Surely, she thought, remembering the hours they'd spent together, he should show some awareness of the passion they'd just shared.

As she made eye contact with him, she felt like a fool. How could she have read so much into one night of love?

It was just as well she hadn't taken the time to share her secret with Sam, she thought sadly. What difference would it have made to him if she'd told him she couldn't have children? He'd never told her he loved her or even cared for her, let alone hinted he wanted to be her husband.

The fact that she was barren could have made a difference to a man who wanted to be her husband. Sam wasn't that man.

She only had herself to blame for deluding herself into thinking Sam loved her. To him, what had taken place last night must have been only sex. He'd been honest when he'd offered to stay on at the ranch for a few days, a week or two at the most, hadn't he?

She added generous helpings of cream and sugar to her coffee and thoughtfully stirred it. If Sam was embarrassed in front of this audience and wanted to remain a friendly stranger, it would break her heart. But then, her heart had been broken before.

She forced herself to smile at Hank. "How did the sleep-out go?"

Hank wiped his lips with the back of his hand and

sent her a dark look. "It didn't. Could have told you camping out wasn't a good idea."

Laura lost her smile. Hank was a cynic, but camping should have been second nature to him by now. "Why not? I remember I loved sitting around a campfire with Dad when I was a little girl."

"Maybe so, but I'll bet you and Jonah didn't spend the night. Campfire or not, it's too damn cold to hunker down in the south pasture. Even the dang sheep were looking for shelter," he added sourly.

"That's why it was a trial run," Laura answered. "Maybe you're right," she added, thinking of how she'd given herself to Sam last night. "I guess memories aren't always real."

Laura looked so forlorn that Sam wanted to take her in his arms and make it better. His own memories of his childhood with his father were probably no more real than hers, but he treasured them just the same. "If it was that cold, you all could have come back here."

Hank's wise old eyes regarded Sam. "Figured you and Laura wanted the chance to be alone."

Sam drained his coffee and reached for the coffee-pot. One way or another, Hank seemed convinced he and Laura belonged together. If only he could be as convinced as Hank.

Laura blushed. "I only stayed home because of my ankle. I had to let you take the children camping.

I'd already promised them a night out around a campfire.''

Hank regarded her through raised eyebrows. "Looks like you're doing okay now."

Laura felt Sam's eyes on her. "I feel much better now. All I really needed was to give my ankle a rest. Sam applied the ice pack and it helped."

Sam sensed Hank was wondering what else he'd done to help heal Laura, but was too polite to come right out and ask. "So where did you all spend the night?"

"Took everyone to the old sheep-herder's cabin and made a fire in the old Ben Franklin stove to keep everyone warm." Hank glanced sourly at Katy before he went on, "Ate beans for dinner and was damn lucky to have 'em."

"It was lots of fun, Miss Laura, honest," Caitlin said, her blue eyes wide with excitement. "Hank, Al and Jim told us stories about the way things were when they were kids. They even taught us the songs they used to sing."

"Songs? What songs?" Sam thought back to his Boy Scout days and the songs they'd sung around the campfire while they toasted marshmallows. Harmless songs like "My Darling Clementine," "Oh, Susanna" and "Down by the Station." From the guilty expression that crossed Hank's face and the way Katy rolled her eyes, Sam was pretty sure the songs had been a little more earthy than the songs he'd remembered.

"Don't even go there," Katy warned with a telling look at Hank. "Heaven help us if the Abbotts ever find out what songs those children heard." Hank properly quelled, she went on, "Right now, folks, it's time for breakfast."

Hank eyed her with a scowl and set his cup in the sink. "Count me out. The boys and I'll take our grub to the bunkhouse."

"Be my guest," Katy answered. She took a bowl out of the cupboard and filled it with six eggs and half of the slab of bacon. "There you are. And don't forget to take the leftover beans with you."

Laura called Hank back before he tramped out of the kitchen. "Wait a minute, Hank. Before you go, try to think of some other ways to entertain the new campers next week."

Sam felt it was his turn to speak before Hank came up with some outlandish idea to get the Abbott kids to herd sheep, or worse. He'd promised to help Laura with the kids, and it looked as if now was the time to pay up. "How about you and me taking the kids on nature walks, Hank? I could teach them a few tricks about photography while you show them the sights. I have some disposable cameras in my SUV we can use."

Hank didn't look any more enthusiastic at the

prospect of hiking with little city slickers than he had about the sleep-out. "You sure you gonna need me?"

Sam smothered a smile. "Yes. Al and Jim can stay here and help Laura and Katy. Since I'm a stranger around here myself, I'll need you as a guide. Wouldn't want to get lost again. No telling what other kind of damage I'd do."

"Well, maybe," Hank replied. He didn't look convinced, but he shrugged and said, "Okay. The boys and I will be at the bunkhouse if you need us."

Sam watched the three leave and recalled how lucky he'd been to get lost a few days ago. He glanced over to where Laura was taking out a frying pan and a griddle from the cupboard and was preparing to make breakfast. In jeans, fuzzy slippers and an old sweatshirt, she not only looked enchanting, she looked more desirable than ever. If only... He forced himself to forget the memories that made his body stir and his mouth turn dry.

"Are you sure you want to get into nature walks?" Laura asked as she cracked eggs into a glass bowl. "You still have that assignment at the spa, don't you?"

"There's no hurry. It's strictly a freelance assignment. I'll call and tell them I'll drop over some time next week." He joined Laura at the stove, carefully sliced bacon and laid out the thick slices on the griddle.

After a few minutes, she asked, "Does that mean you plan on staying on here at the ranch?"

Sam concentrated on adding the cooked bacon to the plates of scrambled eggs Laura handed him before he passed the plates to Katy. "For now. I intended to stick around for a while anyway. I plan to go over to the county courthouse to see if I can get a copy of your adoption papers for you."

At the sound of a car, Katy hurried to the door. "Must be Pete."

Sam hid a grin. Solid pragmatic Katy was as enthusiastic about the sheriff as she was disenchanted with Hank. And judging from the way Pete had been eyeing Katy, the feeling appeared to be mutual. Hank hadn't had to worry.

Laura's heart sank when Pete walked into the kitchen. Judging from the set look on the sheriff's face and his lack of greeting, whatever news he brought with him wasn't going to be good. "Coffee, Pete?"

"No thanks. Just left Josie's. Had my fill of coffee there." He motioned to the Abbott children and glanced meaningfully at Katy. "You might want to take the kids out of here."

One look at the grim expression on the sheriff's face and Katy didn't hesitate. "Come on, kids. Let's go upstairs and clean up. You, too, dumpling,'' she said to Annie as she picked her up. ''We're going upstairs to where it's nice and warm, sweetheart. I'll get the rest of your breakfast after you have a nice warm bath.''

Laura bit her bottom lip and busied herself gathering half-filled plates and empty mugs. No matter how she tried, she couldn't calm the agitated beating of her heart. The little food she'd managed to eat tasted like straw. ''Bad news again, Pete?''

''Depends.'' He glanced at Sam.

''Pete?'' she prodded. ''If it's bad news, I might as well hear about it now.''

Pete nodded reluctantly. ''It's not about you, Laura. Had a long talk with Josie. She says no one actually believes the fool rumor running around that you were never legally adopted. Whoever started the rumor ought to have his head examined and his ass kicked.''

''Hansen?''

Pete cleared his throat. ''Probably. Turns out it's pretty well-known your father left you the ranch and everything else he owned.''

Sam remembered thinking troubles came in pairs, but no way could it continue now that the tax receipts had been found and the townspeople sided with Laura. That left him as the problem. ''What's on your mind, Pete?''

"You."

The single word sent shivers up Sam's spine. "How in hell could I be Laura's problem? Sure, I ran into her fence, but I helped Hank and the boys repair it. I even ordered a new water tower. Ought to be ready next week."

Laura froze in place. A cold heavy undercurrent of tension filled the kitchen. "Sam's right about the fence and the tower. Everything's looking good again, maybe better than before. I didn't ask, but Sam's even paid me room and board for staying here."

When Pete didn't comment, and even though she wanted to stay and back up Sam, Laura felt she had to ask, "Do you want me to leave while you talk to Sam?"

"Think I'll take a cup of that coffee, after all, Laura. Better stick around. You might want to listen to this since it concerns you, too."

"Listen to what?" Sam had had enough. He might not have walked a straight line all his life, but as far as he knew, he'd never done anything illegal. And certainly nothing to warrant the grim look on the sheriff's face.

Pete took the cup of coffee Laura gave him, blew on it and took a deep swallow. "Got a fax into the office from the New York Police Department early this morning."

"So? How does that concern me?"

"They've sent Wanted faxes all over the country. Seems there's a Mrs. Harrison looking for you. She filed a missing-person report."

Sam had a sinking feeling the ceiling was about to fall in on him. "You mean Paige?"

"Yep. That's the lady," Pete said too casually for Sam's peace of mind. "Says you disappeared with a baby girl. Hers."

Sam ran his fingers through his hair and cursed under his breath. In spite of thinking he and his ex had parted on friendly terms, he'd never really understood Paige while they were married, and he understood her even less now. "Hell, I didn't disappear. Paige knew I had a photo shoot assignment at the New Horizons Spa."

"Yeah, well, seems you never showed up."

"I was busy," Sam answered with a sidelong glance at Laura. To his dismay, he saw fear in her eyes. Of him? "As for the baby, she's my daughter, Annie."

"If you have proof of custody that might help."

Sam's felt his stomach drop. If he'd never been in deep trouble before, he was in over his head now. "Well, no, but I didn't take Annie. Not knowingly, anyway. My ex is the one who put her in the back seat of my SUV."

"And you didn't notice?" Pete's eyes turned cold. "Sounds hard to believe."

"Maybe, but I swear it's true," Sam answered. "With the infant seat facing backward, I thought it was part of the seat. Hell, I didn't know Annie was there until I heard her cry. That's when I ran into the fence and took down the water tower." He turned to Laura. "Laura can corroborate my story. Laura?"

She nodded slowly. "That's the way it looked when I found you."

Sam clenched his hands. What had happened to change the warm loving woman who'd spent the night in his arms into a block of ice? "That's the way it *looked?* How about believing me?"

The silence in the kitchen as he waited for an answer grew thick enough to cut with a knife. "I do," Laura finally answered slowly. "That is, I want to believe you…"

"…but you've only known me for a few days." Sam finished for her. "As far as you know, I could have kidnapped Annie. Is that it?"

"No," Laura protested as she remembered the gentle way Sam had held her in his arms last night. And the tender look in his eyes as he made passionate love to her. A memory she would treasure for the rest of her life. "No," she said softly, "the man I know couldn't be a kidnapper. I just don't understand why your wife would file a missing-person report.''

"My *ex-wife*," Sam corrected. "We were divorced almost six months ago. The last time I saw Paige, she'd sold the house I'd given her for a wedding present and packed up everything we owned. Like I said before, I was only there to collect my stuff. At her request, I might add. Paige disliked anything that had to do with photography, and that included me.''

"But she still married you?"

"Yeah, lucky me." Sam said bitterly. "Call it a fatal attraction. No," he said, "that's not fair, but the truth is, the marriage was a mistake for both of us.''

"And how do you account for her putting the baby in the back seat?" Pete held out his cup for Laura to refill. "Don't sound right to me.''

"That's because you don't know Paige," Sam answered. "She was just as obsessed about working as a flight attendant as I was about photography. The note she left pinned to the baby's blanket made it clear she wasn't ready to be a mother. I can show it to you if you like.''

"I like.''

"It's in my duffel bag upstairs." Sam turned on his heel and bounded upstairs to retrieve the note.

"Laura," Pete said softly. "I'm a friend of yours,

but I'm still the law. I wouldn't want you to get hurt in this mess.''

She shook her head. She'd waited a long time to give her heart away, and now she'd given it to Sam. ''I'm afraid it's a little too late.''

Sam strode back into the kitchen and handed Pete the note. ''Well,'' he said when he'd read it, ''at the time, your ex sounds as if she didn't want to keep the baby. Now, it seems, the lady's changed her mind. Otherwise she wouldn't be looking for you.''

''She'll get Annie back over my dead body,'' Sam bit out. ''Being a parent isn't an off-again on-again thing. You can tell Paige for me that Annie's mine now, and I'm going to keep her.''

''Well,'' Pete said after a few minutes' thought, ''I'll keep the note for now. As soon as I get back to the office, I'll fax the NYPD and tell them you've turned yourself in. We'll take it from there.''

''Turned myself in!'' Sam protested. ''Hell, you make it sound as if I'm guilty of something!''

''Sam's right, Pete,'' Laura said. ''Why don't you let him call his wife—his ex-wife? He can talk to her, ask her why she's filed a missing-person report and get her to call it off.'' She turned to Sam. ''You *are* able to talk to her, aren't you?''

''Hell, yes,'' Sam answered. ''We may have married for all the wrong reasons and divorced for the right ones, but the last thing I knew, Paige was still talking to me.''

Pete put down his coffee cup, stood up and reached into his back pocket. ''You can call her from the jailhouse. Until this gets straightened out, you're under arrest for kidnapping.''

''Arrest?'' If Pete hadn't taken a set of handcuffs out of his pocket, Sam would have thought the man was kidding. ''You can't arrest me. I just told you I didn't know Annie was in the back seat!''

''Hold it right there. I might as well tell you that anything you say can and will be held against you. Better save it for the judge.''

When Pete began to read Sam his rights, Laura hopped to her feet in protest. ''Pete! You can't arrest Sam! There's the baby. Who's going to take care of Annie?''

''Yeah, well, that's no problem,'' Pete answered. ''You and Katy are sure qualified to do it if anyone can.'' He motioned to Sam to put his hands behind his back, handcuffed him and took his arm. ''Let's go.''

Sam fought back his anger and looked at Laura. The horror that filled her eyes as she gazed at his handcuffed hands convinced him that no matter what happened to him next, he would never be able to redeem himself in those eyes.

Chapter Twelve

Sam fumed as he angrily paced the narrow jail cell. Hell yes, he intended to talk to his ex about that damn missing-person report. That is, if Paige would stay in one place long enough so he could find her. He was halfway tempted to kill Paige if he ever got his hands on her.

Even the extra telephone call he'd begged Pete to allow him hadn't helped to find her.

His former mother-in-law had told him Paige put most of her belongings in storage and had taken off.

The most the airline Paige worked for was willing to do for him was inform him she'd traded assignments with another attendant and was between flights. After he'd finally lost his temper, they reluctantly agreed to get back to him. In the meantime, they'd offered to take a message.

Why Paige had accused Sam of kidnapping their infant daughter beat the hell out of him.

A delayed sense of guilt at giving up Annie?

A belated desire for the joys of motherhood?

At the thought of Annie, his heart turned over. She must be missing him already. Sure she had Laura, and for that he thanked God, but he was her father. He shuddered at Annie's predicament. Because his predicament was Annie's.

As for Paige, he knew her too well to buy either possible scenario. If it didn't have wings, four engines and flew at thirty-five thousand feet, she wasn't interested.

Until she surfaced and called off the law, his chance of getting out of jail anytime soon on a scale of one to ten was zero.

For a man with wanderlust in his veins, being locked up in an eight-by-ten jail cell where the only amenities were a narrow cot, two blankets and a bucket was sheer torture. To add to his misery, the sounds of automobile traffic coming through the barred window only served to remind him he wasn't going anywhere. And gave him too much time to think.

Apart from being locked behind bars, another thing that really blew his mind big time was the memory of the horrified expression on Laura's face when the sheriff had handcuffed him. And worse yet, looking as if she thought he'd kidnapped Annie and might actually be a fugitive from the law.

Surely she should have sensed in the past few days he'd been at the ranch that he wasn't the type to kidnap his own child.

Loving Laura and the belated realization that the grass wasn't any more photogenic over the next hill than it was at the Lazy E had been a real eye-opener for him. If he hadn't known where he belonged before, after spending the week at the Lazy E, he knew it now.

He cursed his stupidity for not contacting Paige as soon as he discovered the baby in the SUV. If he had, maybe he would still be in Laura's warm embrace, instead of in Pete's custody.

He paced the cold and empty cell, raging inside at being unable to help himself. To add to his despair was the knowledge that as soon as the news of his arrest became known to Josie at the diner and Nate Calhoun over at the Mercantile, it was bound to spread like a prairie fire. Worse yet, the bad publicity might even cause Laura's camp to fold. Or force her to sell the ranch.

Thanks to him, Sam thought bitterly as he paced the concrete floor, Hansen stood a good chance of being able to buy the property without lifting another finger.

The reality made Sam's blood run cold and his temper grow hotter. The giant headache that had started at the sound of the cell door banging closed behind him wasn't helping him think clearly.

"Any luck with the telephone call?" Hands in his pockets, his Stetson hat shoved back on his head, Pete stood on the other side of the iron bars. His smile was friendly, but his eyes were cold.

Friendly, was it? Sam wasn't fooled. After the sheriff had handcuffed him and carted him off to jail like a common criminal? And looked at him as if he'd betrayed their budding friendship? Even the one telephone call he'd allowed him before he'd locked him up had been according to rules, not because of friendship.

Sam shook his head and bit back a rude remark. Pete didn't look like a big-city lawman, but Sam didn't kid himself. If the man had actually been as friendly as he tried to look, he would have listened to reason and he, Sam, wouldn't have found himself behind bars.

"I'm not getting anywhere by myself," he forced himself to admit. "Looks as if I need a lawyer."

"Got one in mind?"

Sam shook his head. "Guess I'll have to take one out of the phone book." He shivered as he glanced around the dismal cell and the single room beyond it that made up the town's jailhouse. "Place could use some improvement. Looks as if it was built a hundred years ago."

"It was," Pete said. "Don't get much crime around here. That is, unless some outsider manages to bring it in," he added with a pointed look at Sam. He headed for his desk. "No use spending money if we don't have to."

"If you're talking about me, you're barking up the wrong tree," Sam growled. "I keep telling you my ex-wife put Annie in my SUV without telling me."

"That's *your* story," Pete answered. "When your wife surfaces, we'll listen to hers. In the meantime, you've got company coming."

Sam's spirits rose like a bird in flight. Maybe he'd misread the look on Laura's face this morning. "Laura? Does she have Annie with her?"

"Nope," Pete replied. He searched the desk drawers. "Don't allow kids inside the jailhouse. Katy called; she's on her way in with lunch. Guess she's afraid I'm keeping you on bread and water."

Katy rushed in in time to hear Pete's comment. She held a covered basket in one hand and a thermos in the other and to Sam looked like an angel of mercy. His mouth watered at the tantalizing scent of freshly baked bread and fresh-from-the-oven cookies that drifted out from under the red-and-white-checked napkin that covered the basket.

"Don't listen to Pete," Katy retorted. "If we hadn't offered to feed you, he would have had that

Josie woman do it.'' She sniffed her disdain. ''You know what diner food tastes like.''

''We?'' Sam asked hopefully, his eyes on the basket. If Laura had taken the time to think of feeding him, maybe he'd read her wrong. ''Did Laura have a hand in this?''

''It was her idea. I'm not much of a cook,'' Katy confessed with an indignant look at Pete that dared him to comment. ''If you were at the ranch trying to prove your innocence, instead of being in here, there wouldn't be a problem with seeing you fed decently.''

Pete's welcome smile grew dim. ''Sam's staying here until I hear back from New York.''

Sam shrugged. With the way his luck was going, he wasn't surprised at the sheriff's refusal to let him out. He couldn't blame the man. Kidnapping was definitely an appalling offense, even if it was your own kid. ''Happens I'm starved, Pete. Never did get my share of breakfast this morning.''

''Open up, Pete!'' Katy demanded with a frosty look at the sheriff. ''This basket isn't going to get into that cell by itself.''

''Not before I check what's inside,'' Pete answered. ''Now don't get riled up,'' he added when Katy started to sputter. ''I've got to check for weapons. Rules are rules.''

Sam lost his cool as he remembered his sinking

gut reaction to the rifle Laura had carried the first time he'd laid eyes on her. Or the time he'd taken the rifle away from her before she used it on Hansen. "Weapons? You've got to be kidding! Outside of that Swiss Army knife you took away from me, I've never touched anything you could call a weapon in my life!"

"Like I said before, rules are rules." Pete lifted the napkin and rummaged inside the basket. "Hmm. Haven't had homemade baked goods for a month of Sundays. What's in the sandwiches?"

"Turkey." Katy's eyes grew wide with incredulity. "Don't tell me you think I'd put a weapon in a sandwich?"

"Now don't get your dander up, Katy," the sheriff said soothingly. "Like I said, rules are rules."

"I don't know why Laura's so goodhearted after what you've done with Sam here," Katy retorted, "but she said one of the sandwiches is for you."

Satisfied no weapons or messages were in the basket, Pete unlocked the door to Sam's cell, handed him the basket and locked the door again. "Give Laura my thanks. You, too, Katy."

Katy sniffed. "If it had been up to me, I wouldn't have given you the time of day."

Sam saw the crestfallen look on the sheriff's face. If ever there was a time to polish the apple, this was it. He passed a sandwich and an apple to Pete.

"Here, enjoy yourself. How long do you think it'll take before you get an answer back from New York?"

"Depends on how soon someone finds your wife and checks out your story. In the meantime, a possible kidnapping isn't exactly a minor offense."

Katy sniffed again.

Sam bit into a sandwich. "I keep telling all of you Paige is my ex-wife. I may be Annie's father, but I'm not married to her mother anymore."

Katy poked Pete in the ribs. "Pete Dolan, do something besides stand there! It's time for Sam to come home. Annie misses him."

Sam chewed his sandwich thoughtfully. The Lazy E with Laura referred to as home and Annie missing him was music to his ears. Too bad he hadn't realized it before now.

"Do what?" Pete protested. "I'm the sheriff around here. I can't just ignore a Wanted bulletin."

"Then the least you could do is see to it Sam gets some help. He can't do much for himself locked up in here."

"Women," Pete muttered as he polished off his sandwich. "I was just going to give Sam the phone book so he could find a lawyer." He headed back to his scarred wooden desk, dug a telephone book out of a drawer and handed it to Sam.

"Well, at least that's something," Katy muttered.

"Hurry it up. Like I said, Annie misses her father."
With a sidelong glance at Sam, she waved goodbye.

Sam's heart took a dive at the mention of his
daughter. A little girl who seemed to have been born
with a smile on her face. He hadn't realized how
much Annie had become a part of him until now.

And then there was Katy. There was something
about the expression on her face that made Sam
wonder if she really believed he was innocent, or if
she was being kind to him for Annie's sake.

"How would you like to shower and shave?"
Pete ambled over to the cell bars.

"Never thought you'd ask," Sam said with a
jaundiced glance at the bucket. He looked around
the one-room jailhouse. "But where?"

"Got a bathhouse out back. Ain't nothing special,
but it works for me." Pete gestured to Sam's wrinkled clothing. "By the way, Katy delivered your
duffel bag with some clean clothing for you."

Sam was tempted to ask the sheriff if he'd
searched the bag for weapons, but he couldn't wait.
If he didn't get out from behind the cell's iron bars
soon, he was going to go stir-crazy. "You going to
let me out long enough to clean up?"

Pete shrugged. "Yeah. Figure you're not going
anywhere without the kid."

Sam had to agree. He might be behind bars, cold,
tired and smelling to high heaven, but thank God he

still had his pride. No way was anyone, especially his little daughter, going to see him looking like the town drunk.

Pete unlocked the door to the cell and indicated a door at the back of the room. "I'll give you twenty minutes. If you don't come out, I'm coming in after you."

Sam dropped the telephone book and headed for the door. The sheriff's version of a bathhouse was a shower, a toilet with a pull chain and a washbasin that had seen better days. Sam shivered, shed his clothing and headed for the shower like a thirsty man who'd stumbled on an oasis in the desert. Thank God the water was hot, he thought as he soaped up and washed his hair.

He thought of the bathroom back at the Lazy E. The aroma of Laura's body wash and the towels where her scent lingered. And most of all Laura's presence on the other side of the door.

The thought of Laura made his body tighten and his head spin. With a muttered curse, he turned on cold water and forced himself to stand under the deluge until his thoughts turned away from the night he and Laura had spent together.

Until he was cleared of the kidnapping charge, he intended to keep his thoughts pure and on business.

Twenty minutes later, feeling like a new man and

fresh with resolve to end this farce once and for all and soon, he made his way back into his cell.

He turned to the telephone book. The chances of finding a lawyer in the Yellow Pages didn't look very good. But he no choice.

Pete called from his desk. "If you can't find someone in there, I can call my brother, Russ. Maybe he can come up with some ideas."

"Ideas? What kind of ideas?"

"Russ is a lawyer up in Grand Junction. But," Pete added with a grim expression on his face, "I want this understood. I'm doing it for Laura, not for you."

Sam nodded at the curt message. Somewhere in the past few days, he'd sensed Pete had warmed to him. Maybe even respected him. Things looked a hell of a lot different now. "Sorry to hear that. I was kind of hoping we'd become friends."

"Not after a charge like possible kidnapping. And especially not after what it could mean to Laura." With a look at Sam that rocked him on his heels, Pete picked up the telephone, turned his back and started punching in a telephone number.

Sam dropped to the cot and began counting iron bars again to keep his cool. Paige had a lot of explaining to do.

The connection made, Sam could hear Pete talking to his brother on the telephone. Snatches of conversation were clear.

"...showed up at Laura's place with a baby he claims is his..."

"...no, Laura didn't know him. You might say they met by accident..."

"...says he's a photographer, but I ain't seen any camera..."

"...almost arrested him for threatening someone with an old rifle..."

"...yeah, he fits the description. But he thinks he has an alibi..."

The story Pete seemed to be relating into the telephone sounded bizarre, even to Sam, who'd lived it. If he'd been Russell Dolan, he wouldn't have believed his story, either.

Sam was sure he might have had a prayer of convincing everyone he was a genuine photographer if he'd taken the time to contact the New Horizons Spa after the accident. Just having cameras with him didn't seem to cut the mustard. As for his finding Annie in the back seat of his SUV, so far it was his word against his ex-wife's.

Sam tried hard to ignore Pete's telephone conversation. All he could think about was the look on Laura's face the last time he'd seen her. And how stupid he'd behaved by not responding to the sparkle in her eye before Pete showed up.

Why had he been so afraid of showing her how happy she'd made him?

Why had he been so afraid of commitment when he'd known by then that Laura was the woman for him?

The not-so-simple truth had been the memory of his traumatic divorce and Paige's comments. His uneasy feeling that somewhere along the line he'd failed to be the husband and father he should have been. That, even now, his fear he wouldn't be able to cure his wanderlust.

There was no use wondering what he would have done, not now. First he had to convince the law he was an innocent man.

No sooner had Pete hung up the phone than more of Sam's worst fears were realized. Hansen, immaculate in summer whites, strode into the jailhouse. A smirking Magraw, unshaven and looking as rumpled as ever, trailed behind him.

"Heard there's a Wanted bulletin out on you, Harrison," Hansen said as he stopped in front of the iron bars. "Not such a big shot without that rifle, are you?"

Pete rushed over. "Now see here, Hansen. You're not allowed in here—not unless I say so. And I ain't said so. So take yourself and that man of yours out of here. Now!"

Hansen stood his ground. "This is public property. I'm not leaving until I've had my say."

"Let the man stay, Pete," Sam said between set lips. "I want to hear what he has to say." From the triumphant look on Hansen's face, Sam had a strong feeling Hansen thought he held the winning hand, that he would get the Lazy E dirt cheap. As far as Sam was concerned, Hansen wasn't going to win a damn thing. Not now, not ever.

What really began to worry him was that Laura was bound to go head-to-head with Hansen sooner or later. Maybe sooner if she had her way. Maybe even wind up in jail for threatening Hansen. Worse yet, she might go after the man with that old rifle she had in the barn. An old rifle that may not be able to shoot straight but could blow up in her face.

These damn iron bars kept him from doing something for her.

One way or another, Hansen was going to have to understand it was hands off Laura and the Lazy E. All Sam needed was for Hansen to come one step closer to the cell bars.

The cold cell grew even colder as Sam waited for Hansen to drop the other shoe. It didn't take long. Only this time it was Magraw who spoke up.

"Just you wait until the morning newspaper comes out with you in the headlines," the man said slyly. "You and that woman of yours are gonna find you aren't as smart as you think you are."

Sam looked over Magraw's shoulder at Pete in time to see the sheriff shake his head. If the sheriff hadn't let out the news Sam was in jail on a suspected kidnapping charge, who had?

"How did the newspaper get wind of my being in here?" he asked. As if he hadn't already learned Magraw seemed to be in on everything that went on in Montgomery County.

"I have my sources," Magraw said proudly. "I—"

"Shut up, Harry," Hansen broke in coldly. "Your tongue wags on both ends."

When Magraw subsided with a muttered threat, Hansen turned his attention back to Sam. "There is a way to stop this, you know."

"No, I don't know," Sam replied, his hands in his pockets to keep from reaching through the bars and strangling Hansen. "Why don't you fill me in?"

"All you have to do is persuade Ms. Evans to sell out to me. She has nothing to lose and everything to gain if she does."

"And if I don't?"

"Then the local newspapers and every paper in the country, for that matter, are going to hear about that Wanted bulletin. That she's been harboring a criminal. And when they do, Ms. Evans's chances of running a camp will be slim to none. No one is going to want to have their children associated with her. Or with you, either.''

Sam took a deep breath and made a silent vow. If he'd ever seriously thought of taking Annie and getting out of Laura's life, the thought was gone now. Laura needed someone to protect her interests, and that someone was going to be him. Where their relationship went from there remained to be seen.

''You're quick to assume I have influence over the lady.''

Hansen smiled a smile that didn't reach his eyes and left Sam little doubt as to what he was thinking. ''From what I hear about the two of you sleeping together, Mr. Harrison, plenty.''

Sam lunged forward and grasped the bars. ''If I wasn't in here, you'd be minus a few teeth and laughing on the other side of your mouth, Hansen.''

''But you are in here, aren't you,'' Hansen said, satisfaction oozing from his voice. ''And that's where it looks like you're going to stay for a long long time. So how about going along with me? I'll make it worth your while. Oh, and by the way, too bad your little girl has a jailbird for a father. That is, if she really is your child and not someone you kidnapped.''

Hansen was so set on taunting Sam that he forgot

himself and took that last step that brought him within Sam's range.

Furious, Sam brought his hands out of his pockets and reached between the bars for Hansen's neck. Pete lunged forward to stop him before he made contact. "That's enough. Get out of here, Hansen. And take your dirt with you. And as for Sam being in here for any length of time, that's none of your business."

Obviously shaken at Sam's attempt to attack him, Hansen nodded curtly and strode out of the jail-house. With one last glance at Sam's face, Magraw beat him to the door.

Sam forced himself to pull back. When he was finally able to draw a normal breath, he turned to Pete. "Does that mean you finally believe me?"

"Can't say that I do, not yet, anyway." Pete looked embarrassed. "The truth is, I *was* beginning to like you, even respect you. Even thought for a time there you and Laura would make it. But a kid-napping? Gotta admit, I'm disappointed in you."

"I told you I didn't kidnap Annie! Her mother put her in the car without my knowledge."

"Yeah, well, Russell said your story sounded too bizarre *not* to be true. Said no one could make up a story like that. But don't get your hopes up. You're not going to go anywhere without your ex-wife admitting to the NYPD that she put the baby in your car.''

By now Sam was so frustrated he could hardly talk. ''And how about the morning-newspaper headlines? If the reason I'm in jail ever comes out in print, it's not going to be pretty. Hansen's right—it sure isn't going to do Laura any good, either.''

Pete frowned. ''Hell, Magraw's sources aren't any better than mine. Alan Howard, the editor of the newspaper, and I go back a long way. As a matter of fact, we went to school together. I'll ask him to hold off for a day. Chances are he'll do it if I promise to give him the whole story as soon as it's settled.''

Sam nodded slowly. He was relieved that Pete could get his friend to keep the story quiet for now.

Sam's spirits rose when the jailhouse door opened and Laura came in. The fact that the man with her carried a briefcase told Sam the man was probably a lawyer or an official of some sort.

''Laura?'' Sam grasped the bars that separated him from the woman he'd prayed to see. The expression on her pale face tore at Sam's heart. He would have given anything not to have been the one to put the sadness there. ''Is Annie okay?''

''She's fine,'' Laura answered. ''I left her with Katy. She and the Abbott kids are having a picnic.''

"Thanks for coming," Sam said softly. "I can't tell you how much it means to me."

Laura nodded curtly, averted her face and spoke to Pete. "I brought Harvey Thomas. He's agreed to listen to Sam's story and see if he can help."

"Good thing, too," Pete replied as he shook the lawyer's hand. "Thought you'd retired or I would have suggested you. Harrison doesn't know any lawyers around here who'd be able and willing to handle a case like this." He picked up the keys to Sam's cell. "Say the word, Harvey, and I'll let you into the cell with the prisoner. You can talk as long as you want."

Prisoner! Cell! Sam's heart plunged as Laura's face grew paler. He wanted to take her in his arms and assure her that everything was bound to turn out okay sooner or later, to ask her to believe in him. The last thing he'd expected was for her to see him behind bars.

With a nod and a glance at Sam, Harvey Thomas said, "In case you're wondering, gentlemen, I may be retired, but I'm still a member of the Colorado bar. I've agreed to listen to your story, Mr. Harrison. But before we begin, you'll have to formally appoint me to represent you."

Pete's prodding shook Sam out of his preoccupation with the way Laura was avoiding meeting his eyes. "Sam, you gotta say the words."

"I'd like you to represent me, Mr. Thomas," Sam said, his eyes on Laura. "If you don't mind, I'd like to have a minute alone with Laura before we get started."

To his dismay, Laura ignored him. She shook hands with the lawyer. "Let me know if you need anything, Harvey. I'll be at the ranch."

"Laura?" Sam tried again, grasping the iron bars. Before it was too late he had to tell her that his traveling days were over. That he'd come to realize he wanted to put down roots and be a loving husband and father. He wanted to tell her of the role he hoped she'd play in his life. "Stay a minute, please. I have to talk to you before you go."

"I'm sorry," she said softly with a quick glance at him that broke his heart. "I'll keep Annie with me until her future is decided. As for me, I don't want to see you again."

The jailhouse door slammed shut behind her.

An uneasy silence filled the jail. While Pete and Harvey gazed at Sam in silent sympathy, Sam could hear music coming through the open window of an automobile outside on the street. He grimaced as the car moved on and the music faded.

He was devastated by the way Laura had refused to listen to him. To even look at him. If it hadn't been for Harvey Thomas and the pressing need to tell the lawyer his side of the story, he would have begged Pete to call Laura back. At least long enough to hear him out.

Only half listening, Sam answered the lawyer's questions. He related Paige's request that he come and take the last of his belongings she'd packed and had ready for him. Told him how startled he'd been when he'd heard Annie cry in the back seat of his SUV. And about the resulting accident that had sent him careering into Laura's fence and water tower.

All through the interview, Sam couldn't stop being aware of the iron bars that surrounded him. He felt despair at being in jail for however long it took for Paige to surface. And anguish over Laura's parting words that suggested he might lose his precious little daughter.

It wasn't only Annie he stood to lose. It looked as if he'd also lost Laura, the love of his life.

Chapter Thirteen

Laura could hardly see through her tears. It was a good thing the old ranch truck seemed to find its way home without her, or she would have been lost. The way Sam was now lost to her.

She couldn't afford to think of herself as the new woman she'd become under Sam's loving embrace. Or to remember the low velvety sound of his voice, the taste of his lips on hers or the strength in the arms that had held her close. She may have been seduced by Sam once, but never again, she vowed.

She drove past herds of sheep grazing in lush green pastures, inhaled the scent of spring wildflowers and the air cleansed by the recent rain. Even though she was surrounded by the familiar countryside she loved from the first day she'd come to live at the Lazy E ranch, her heart still ached. All she could see was the stricken look in Sam's eyes when she'd told him she never wanted to see him again.

It hadn't been Pete arresting and handcuffing Sam that had disturbed her, although Lord knew, the sight had shocked her to the depths of her soul. Nor seeing Sam behind bars. She'd always known in her heart of hearts he'd told her the truth about finding Annie in the back seat of his SUV.

Telling the man she loved she never wanted to see him again had been the most difficult decision of her life. She hadn't made it because of the realization Sam had been a stranger until just over a week ago; no, she'd made it because he was a self-confessed rolling stone. Even without Sam under suspicion for kidnapping, his continued presence on the Lazy E might well jeopardize the children's camp she needed to hold on to the ranch. Without it, she didn't have a prayer.

There was also her responsibility to Katy, who'd given up her job at the hospital. There was Hank, a friend who'd been on the ranch forever and who had no other home.

All these things had finally clinched her decision to cut her ties to Sam before it was too late. These, and the reason he'd given her for his divorce: his obsession with photography that took him away from home.

She remembered too well from years in foster homes what being lonely meant. There was no way she could bring herself to settle down with a man who might not be there when she needed him.

She consoled her heart with the thought that, with Harvey Thomas's help, it would only be a matter of time before Sam's ex-wife was located. Surely the record could be straightened out in a matter of days, and Sam would be free to move on. But not home to her.

She turned into the road leading to the ranch and pulled up in front of the house. To her dismay, Katy, with a smiling Annie in her arms dressed in a daffodil-yellow romper suit, was waiting for her.

"How did it go?" Katy asked as Laura trudged up the steps.

"Sam hired Harvey as his lawyer."

"I wasn't talking about Harvey and you know it," Katy said gently. "I was talking about Sam."

"He seemed to be all right." Annie, the bright spot in Laura's life, chose that moment to reach out her little arms for Laura. Unable to resist and knowing that Annie would be lost to her in a matter of days, Laura gathered the baby in her arms and hugged her close.

"Did you get a chance to talk with Sam?" Katy persisted.

"No." Laura answered. "He wanted to talk, but I didn't want to listen. I did tell him I never wanted to see him again. And no," she added when Katy started to protest, "it wasn't because he's in jail among other reasons. It was because the last thing I need in my life is a man who's a rolling stone."

"Come on, Laura," Katy scolded. "Did you ever stop to think Sam might have had a reason not to put down roots? And that it was already too late for him to change by the time he found out about Annie? Maybe the only sin Sam committed was being human."

"I don't know and I'm too afraid to find out," Laura said as she buried her lips in Annie's golden-brown hair, a color the baby shared with her father. Unable to have a child of her own, little Annie had been Laura's chance to be a mother. Just as Sam had been her chance to become a wife.

The thought of losing Annie was bad enough; the thought of never seeing Sam again almost broke her heart.

The shouts of the Abbott children running out of the barn trying to round up a stray ewe kept Laura from having to tell Katy more. How could she have explained saying no to Sam when her heart yearned to say yes?

"What in heaven's name is going on?" Laura asked as Hank, Jim and Al came charging out of the barn after the children.

"Hank's been trying to get the ewe to bond with the little bum lamb he found the other day." Katy shrugged. "I told him it was useless. Just because the old fool's decided the ewe is the little one's mother, it looks to me as if bonding isn't going to happen."

Laura touched the tiny dimple in Annie's chin with a gentle forefinger and smiled into the baby's sparkling brown eyes. "We've both learned by now that becoming a mother doesn't always guarantee she'll bond with her baby, does it?" *Or Annie's mother wouldn't have given her to Sam.*

"Annie's a good example," Katy said as they watched the melee going on in the yard. She looked out over the horizon toward Montgomery and smiled faintly. "On the other hand, the baby just might have lucked out with a father like Sam."

"You like Sam a lot, don't you?"

Katy gazed at Laura quizzically. "I do. I'm pretty sure he's not a kidnapper. I do worry, though, about what might happen to him when Harvey Thomas hears Sam defended your right to refuse to sell the ranch to Hansen. With the end of a rifle, no less."

Laura was taken aback. "Good Lord! I'd forgotten all about the rifle incident. You don't think Hansen is going to press charges, do you?"

"Might," Katy answered as they walked to the barn. "Let's just hope Sam doesn't get jail time for threatening Hansen. If he does, it sounds to me as if you're going to have to see Sam again, if only to testify in his defense.''

"Maybe I should apologize to Hansen, try to reason with him.'' Laura shuddered at the thought, but she would do it if it could keep Sam from having to do jail time.

Katy sniffed. "Not on your life.'' A frown creased her forehead. "What I don't like about all this is the effect Sam's being in jail now has had on you. You haven't been yourself since Pete took Sam into custody.'' She stopped in midstride and waited until Laura stopped beside her. "Tell me the truth, Laura. You can't possibly believe Sam kidnapped the baby, can you?''

"No.'' Laura answered softly. She gently removed the strand of her hair Annie had grasped and kissed the baby's fingers. "It's a future with Sam I don't trust.''

"Maybe Sam would put away his walking boots if you gave him a reason to stay.''

Laura shook her head. "Maybe, but that's not the only reason I can't think of a future with him. I haven't told him I'm unable to have children of my own. And even if I could, I wouldn't want a child to have an absentee father.''

"So tell Sam, talk things over with him,'' Katy urged. "Maybe having more children isn't important to him. After all, he has Annie. And maybe now that he's met you, he's given up the idea of being a wandering man.''

"What's done is done," Laura answered. "I can't go back now. I'll think about what to do if and when the time comes.''

"I WASN'T GOING to let Hansen hassle Laura, or Magraw, either," Sam said stubbornly later that day when his lawyer brought up the incident about the rifle that Laura had related to him. "Since I had no way of knowing the rifle couldn't fire, I wasn't going to let her shoot him, either. Pete knows I'm telling the truth about the rifle.''

"Maybe so, but he wasn't there when you threatened Magraw with it," Harvey said. "Even if Pete backs you up, do yourself a favor—try not to antagonize Hansen any more than you already have, or you might find yourself behind bars for a long time." Harvey closed his notepad and pocketed his pen. "First things first. If we're going to get the Wanted bulletin canceled, we're going to have to find your ex.''

"Good luck," Sam muttered. "Hope you have better ideas on how to find Paige than I did.''

"One," the lawyer said quietly. "It's been my experience that there's only one reason a person files a missing-person report—they're looking for someone. Since it appears to me that for some reason, the ex-Mrs. Harrison was looking for you, she might have left a message somewhere." He paused to consider. "Where do you suppose that somewhere might be?"

Sam searched his memory. He'd been in so many places in so short a time he couldn't think clearly anymore. Had he told Paige where his next stop was going to be before she put the baby in the back seat?

Surely she wouldn't have put Annie in his SUV if she hadn't thought Sam's next destination would be close so he'd find the baby soon.

One thought led to another. Lightbulbs flashed. The New Horizons Spa!

He recalled promising Paige he'd stop by to pick up his belongings on his way to the spa. If he hadn't been detoured by the accident, he'd be at the spa now, instead of behind bars.

On the other hand, if not for the accident, he wouldn't have met Laura.

He cursed under his breath before he realized the accident had been a double-edged sword. That meeting with Laura had been one of the best things that had ever happened to him. That, and his daughter, Annie.

"The New Horizons Spa," Sam excitedly told Harvey. "I told Paige I was on my way there to do a photo session for a magazine layout. I just never got there."

"Sounds like a good place to start." Harvey pushed back his hat, and called to Pete to let him out of the cell. "I'll get back to you later this afternoon or tomorrow morning."

"Does that mean I have to spend another night in this hotel?" Sam asked bitterly.

"Could have taken you up to Grand Junction," Pete said with a laconic shrug as he unlocked the cell door. "They're not as friendly as I am."

Sam reluctantly nodded at the reminder. He shook hands with Harvey and stood back to let the lawyer leave. When the door clanged shut behind him, Sam's spirits took a dive.

Until he realized that if the lawyer's hunch was right and Paige had actually left a message at the spa for him to call her, he might be home free soon. The most he would have to spend behind bars was another day or two. Unless, for some fool reason or another, she still pressed charges.

Until then, he had a lot of thinking to do. Primarily figuring out why he'd spent most of his adult life on the move. Even after Paige had told him he was going to be a father.

How could he have wanted a family and then run away from the family he already had at the same time?

What had he been afraid of?

The answer came as swiftly as a bolt of lightning.

Even after Annie had been conceived on one of his infrequent trips home, he'd been afraid to put down roots. Let alone be a full-time father. Now he was forced to search his soul.

He realized he'd subconsciously been afraid something might happen to him. That he might leave a grieving child behind, the same way his father had left him.

He thought back to the last time he'd seen his father alive. They'd been playing basketball, shooting for the hoop attached to the front of the garage, when his father's ride to work had shown up. His father had tossed the basketball to him with a backward flip, saluted and waved goodbye. Eight hours later he'd been told his father had been killed by a hit-and-run driver. He'd never forgotten the deep loss.

He fought back a sob as he realized that although he'd loved his father and wanted to be a family man like him, he'd never forgiven his father for leaving him.

Now was the time to forgive his father. Now he had a chance to be the father to Annie that his own father had tried to be to him.

HE SHOULD HAVE KNOWN a telephone call wasn't going to spring him.

After another cold night on a cot, Sam felt stiff

and sore all over. The fact that Pete had also spent the night on a cot on the other side of the iron bars wasn't comforting. The sheriff was getting paid to guard him. To add to his misery, Katy hadn't made her good Samaritan call this morning.

"Breakfast," Pete announced as he ambled into view. He handed Sam a white takeout box and a covered plastic cup of coffee. To a cold and unhappy man, the smell of bacon and eggs and hot coffee was nirvana. Even if it came from Josie's Diner, instead of Laura's kitchen.

"What did Josie say when you asked for takeout?" Sam reached for the plastic fork Pete handed him. He would have liked a knife to cut the bacon, but it looked as if knives were out. He opened the lid and gazed at Josie's "Early Morning Special." No jam, but at least the toast was buttered.

"No problem. Told her I had a vagrant in here spending the night out of the cold. She was just as happy for him to be in here than holed up in the diner trying to keep warm."

Sam gestured to Pete's cot. "Spend a lot of time in here?"

"Only when I have to." Pete went back to the desk and opened the box that held his own breakfast. "Like I said, we don't have much big-time crime around here. In fact, you're the first."

Sam shrugged, sat down on the cot and dug into

his meal. The coffee was only lukewarm, but strong enough to have a kick in it. A second cup, he realized unhappily when the cup was empty, was obviously out.

"How about a shower and a shave?" Sam asked when he finished breakfast. "It will help pass the time."

"Shower yes, shave no," Pete answered. "Same rules as yesterday. Twenty minutes. There's more of your clothes in a shopping bag under the sink." He tossed his box and cup into the trash and unlocked the door to Sam's cell.

Frustrated at being treated like a criminal, Sam scratched at the dark fuzz on his cheeks and headed for the shower. Instead of feeling relieved at the prospect of a hot shower, he was disgusted and mad as hell. For the first time in his life, his future wasn't in his hands.

Three hours later his lawyer showed up. "I hit the jackpot," Harvey announced as he came in the door. "Seems your ex left a telephone number where she could be reached in case you showed up."

"You mean you reached Paige?" Sam's spirits lifted.

"Didn't try. Passed the good news to the New York Police Department that you were in here, with a request they get back to Pete as soon as they connect with your ex. When they told me Pete had already informed them you were here, I told them I was your lawyer and gave them your side of the story.''

''And?''

''They'll get back to me as soon as they talk to the lady. The rest is up to her.''

Sam's spirits sank. Surely Paige would call off the law once he had a chance to speak to her. ''Now what? Does that mean I can get out of here soon?''

Harvey traded glances with Pete. ''Any new bulletins come in?''

''Nope.'' Pete gestured to the fax machine and the computer on a table behind his desk. As far as Sam was concerned, they were the only signs the Montgomery County Sheriff's Department had joined the twenty-first century.

Sam spent the rest of the day thinking about Annie. Thinking about Laura, feeling his guts tied in knots. So he wouldn't go crazy, he spent the time reading an almanac. By the time supper rolled around, he was able to predict the local weather for the year, estimated rainfall and what crops would thrive under the La Niña conditions they were currently experiencing. All good information if he'd been a rancher, he thought wryly. Useless to a freelance photojournalist.

His chances of persuading Laura to stand still long enough for him to apologize and to promise her the future she deserved were about as good as a snowball's in hell.

He was saved from haranguing Pete when the fax machine started to sputter and the telephone rang. Pete gazed at the fax machine and reached for the telephone. He listened closely, nodded, glanced at Sam and hung up.

The hair on the back of Sam's neck started to prickle. Cold shivers ran up and down his spine. If he'd ever been sure of anything in his life, he was sure that the fax sputtering out of the machine and the telephone call concerned him.

"What's up?"

"The NYPD just wanted me to know they've connected with your ex. She's promised to come in tomorrow morning to talk to them."

"Talk? Just talk?" Frustrated, Sam grasped the cold iron bars and squeezed until his knuckles turned white. "How about her calling off the Wanted bulletin so I can get out of here?"

"The NYPD can't do anything unless she shows up in person, makes a statement and signs it," Pete answered. "She made a pretty serious charge. 'Course, if it's not true, seems to me she has a lot of explaining to do."

"Maybe," Sam muttered. "Then again, maybe not. To give her some credit, maybe she's concerned about Annie."

He rubbed the spot on the back of his head where a headache had kicked in. He'd told himself before, told Katy, too, that he was ready to accept some of the blame for his divorce. Now he had to find a way to explain it to Laura. To tell her he'd finally learned the meaning of commitment.

"Think the lady is out to get even with you?"

Sam shook his head. "No. Paige didn't seem to hold the divorce against me. In fact, she was more eager to split than I was. No way would she try to get back at me."

He gazed helplessly at Pete. Somehow he had to make the man understand he had to make up for the mess he'd made of things. Not only with Paige. With Laura, too. "You've got to let me try to get hold of Paige. I need to talk to her."

Pete shook his head. "You've already had more telephone calls than any one person's entitled to."

"Yeah, I know," Sam said, "rules are rules. But sure as hell they can sometimes be broken."

Sam said a silent prayer as Pete studied him thoughtfully. If the sheriff had ever liked or respected him before, surely he would allow him the telephone call that, if it didn't set him free, at least would give him a chance to clear up any misunderstanding.

Pete opened his desk and took out a sheet of paper. "Okay. For what it's worth, here's the telephone number the spa gave Harvey. One call, and that's it. After that, we wait.''

The way Sam's luck had been running, he wasn't surprised to find Paige had moved on. Word was, she was on her way back to New York City. Now the only thing he could do was wait.

He threw himself across his cot and covered his eyes with his arm. The only sound that broke the silence surrounding him were the crickets outside the jailhouse window. The rhythmic sound seemed to soothe his soul as he drifted off to sleep. But nothing soothed him more than the voice he heard in his dream.

''Sam?''

Sam stirred in his sleep. Laura? This had to be a dream, and if it was, he didn't want to wake up. Not until he'd talked to the real Laura. Had a chance to tell her how much he'd learned about himself in the past few days. Told her he loved her and wanted to be her husband.

LAURA WAS OUTSIDE pulling weeds from the vegetable garden beside the house. Annie, in her infant seat, was beside her playing with her rattle. Fancy chased butterflies.

''Laura?'' a familiar voice said softly. ''I'm *home*.''

Laura's heart skipped a beat. Fearing she heard

the beloved voice only in her thoughts, she sighed and tackled another weed.

"Laura," the voice persisted, "I've come home to you and Annie."

She sat back on her heels and shaded her eyes from the sun. Sam, tall and smiling, stood beside her. "How...?"

Sam pulled her to her feet. "Paige came through. Seems all she wanted was to make sure Annie was okay. A little late, but what the heck, maybe being a mother *is* in the woman's genes."

He gazed into Laura's eyes and outlined her lips with a gentle finger. "I didn't know if you wanted me here, but I had to come back and tell you how much I wanted to be your husband. To be the man beside you in bed when you close your lovely eyes at night. And the man beside you when you open your eyes in the morning."

"Oh, Sam," Laura cried, "I thought you were only a dream." She flung her arms around his neck. "You don't know how much I've missed you. How much I've wanted you to hold me, make love to me." She met his lips with all the passion in her, drowned in his kiss, his touch, his voice.

"I'm real," he answered with a shaky laugh as he brushed Laura's cheek with his lips. "I'm real, and if you give me a chance, I'd love to show you just how real I am."

Epilogue

One year later.

Sam stood in the doorway of the barn with his arm around his wife looking across the yard. The object of their interest was eighteen-month-old Annie, who toddled around the hard-packed earth chasing a little lamb.

"Annie is a miracle, isn't she?" Laura smiled up into her husband's eyes. "I'm so happy Paige decided to leave Annie in your custody."

"Yeah," Sam answered. "Paige frightened the life out of me. I was beginning to think I'd be in jail for life. On the other hand," he said, "I learned to let go of the past and to appreciate miracles. You and Annie."

"For that matter, all children are miracles, aren't they?" Laura gazed back at Sam with stars in her eyes.

Sam nodded. His eyes lit up as he pulled her close

and planted a kiss on the rosy lips that never failed to fascinate him. "You bet. And that includes our little Jake. By the way, I'd like to remind you that today marks one year since Paige had the Wanted bulletin called off. Ironic, isn't it," he added, "when all she wanted was to make sure Annie was okay. Can't complain, though. My winding up in jail gave me a chance to realize how much you and I belong together." He kissed Laura again. "It's also eleven months from the day you married me."

"What makes you think I'd forget an important anniversary like that?" Laura asked. "Or that I could forget another miracle—our son asleep in the cradle upstairs?"

Her eyes were shining as she reached up and pulled Sam's head down to meet hers. "That was kiss number two thousand. This one," she said softly, "is kiss two thousand and one. To thank you for agreeing to adopt little Jake."

"Keeping count of kisses?" Sam said with a broad smile. When Laura nodded, Sam bent over and planted another tender kiss on her lips. "Well, as long as you're counting, here's another one that makes kiss number two thousand and two."

"Sam, everyone will notice." Laura laughed softly and gazed around the yard where Hank had finally corralled the new little bum lamb. He was kneeling with the lamb in his arms and showing it to Annie.

"If they don't know how much I love you, they're blind." He sighed regretfully and straightened. "Today is another anniversary—the beginning of camp. Unless I'm mistaken, six more little miracles are going to show up in another hour or two."

Laura giggled. "I never thought I'd hear you call the Abbott children little miracles. Caitlin, yes, but not the boys. They're a handful."

"Laura, my sweet," Sam said with a broad smile, "I like kids, the more the better. In fact, I can't wait to give Annie and Jake some siblings."

Laura sobered. "You don't mind that I can't give you children of your own?"

"You're mistaken, sweetheart," Sam answered. "You've already given me a child by arranging Jake's adoption." He held Laura close and inhaled the spicy scent that reminded him of the many showers they'd taken together. And of the loving they shared.

"Each little miracle we add to our family *is* a child of *our* own," he whispered into her ear. "I didn't ask you to marry me in order to have more children. I asked you to marry me because I love you and want to spend the rest of my life being your husband."

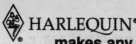

*Together for the first time
in one Collector's Edition!*

New York Times bestselling authors

Barbara Delinsky

Catherine Coulter Linda Howard

Forever Yours

**A special trade-size volume containing three
complete novels that showcase the passion,
imagination and stunning power that these
talented authors are famous for.**

Coming to your favorite retail outlet in December 2001.

HARLEQUIN®
Makes any time special®

PHFY

Coming in December from